Dr. Joseph R. Valinoti
372 Main Street
Apt. 308
Port Washington, NY 11050

Port Harbor
Condo Library

The
Ship's
Clock

Also by Catherine M. Rae

Brownstone Facade
Julia's Story
Sarah Cobb
Afterward

The Ship's Clock

A Family Chronicle

Catherine M. Rae

St. Martin's Press New York

The section concerning the invention of suspenders on pages 24–25 is based on a true story as reported in *As You Pass By* by Kenneth Dunshee (New York: Hastings House, 1952), pages 96–97.

Design by Judith A. Stagnitto

Production Editor: Suzanne Magida

Production Manager: Kathy Fink

Library of Congress Cataloging-in-Publication Data

Rae, Catherine M.
      The ship's clock / Catherine M. Rae.
          p. cm.
    ISBN 0-312-09386-1
    I. Title.
PS3568.A355S54   1993
813'.54—dc20   93-7432
                                       CIP

First Edition: June 1993

10 9 8 7 6 5 4 3 2 1

For Gene

I am indebted to Penelope Colby and Jacqueline Stevens for their help in the preparation of this book.

The
Ship's
Clock

Part
I

Ham‑burg, 1810

A cold January wind, sweeping unimpeded across the River Elbe, rattled the small leaded windows of the ground-floor office of Mesner and Sons, Shipping Merchants, where two young men listened with attention not unmixed with dismay as the head of the company outlined his plans for their futures.

"But, Father, I had planned to marry, and—" Philip, the older son, began when Franz Mesner paused for a moment.

"It makes no difference what your personal desires are, Philip," the senior Mesner said brusquely, leaning forward in his high-backed chair and staring hard at the young man sitting on the opposite side of the heavy oak table. "In this matter you will obey my wishes to the letter. One week from today you will sail on the *Ingrid* for America, where you will look after our interests.

"Trade with that country is increasing rapidly, and I intend that the firm of Mesner and Sons shall have its proper share. As you know, Albert Pfeil, our agent there, is old, and will soon have to retire. Therefore I want you, Philip, now that you are twenty-five years of age, to work under him until I see fit to put you in charge at that end—a few years hence, most likely. Originally I had planned to send Johann Eckstrom to work under Pfeil, but recently his health has not been good, and I am afraid to take a chance on him. But you, Philip, are young and strong, and I shall expect you to work hard to make the name of Mesner and Sons famous in American shipping. Pfeil is merely an agent, but you are a Mesner, and as such will be head of the New York branch of the firm. Do you understand me?"

"I understand perfectly, Father," Philip replied, turning away from the compelling gaze of the older man and glancing out at the gray waters of the river. "Yes, I understand you, but I do not like to—"

"Enough!" shouted Franz Mesner, flushing angrily and banging a fist on the table. "What you do or do not like is of no importance! The welfare of this company is of every importance, and I demand your loyalty to it!

"As for you, Hans," he continued more calmly, sitting back in his chair and turning to his younger son, "in addition to your duties here you will concentrate on the study of the English language for one year, by which time you should be fluent enough to become our agent in Liverpool. Philip already speaks better English than any of us, and will have no trouble dealing with the Americans."

"England? Father, I—"

"Yes, Hans, England. And had I more sons instead of a household of useless females I would send them to ports all over the globe. Ah, then Mesner and Sons would be a power to be reckoned with!"

For a few minutes the hard, stern features seemed to soften, and the dark brown eyes to sparkle, as if they were witnessing a scene in which hundreds of ships bearing the Mesner name were ploughing the sea-lanes of the world.

A low, whirring sound broke the silence that had fallen upon the room, and all three men fastened their eyes on the clock that had been set amidship in the small model of a sixteenth-century sailing vessel. Fascinated as children looking into a toy shop window, they watched as the mechanism of the clock set into motion tiny figures on the deck when the hour hand pointed to twelve.

Franz Mesner never lost an opportunity to inform any visitor or business acquaintance that the long-ago ancestor who had commissioned the clock had specified that each of the small wooden figures represent a member of the newly formed firm of Mesner and Sons, the captain, of course, being Old Mesner himself.

"And it has been in the family all these years," Franz would say, "representing among other things the success of a family in the world of shipping over the centuries. A veritable treasure!"

It is entirely out of character, Philip thought as the silvery chimes began to sound, for a man of business as ruthless as my father to wax romantic, and to take such delight in what is no more than a plaything. Yet he sets more store by the Ship's Clock than he does by his children. He'd rather lose one of us, especially one of the girls, than that timepiece. And as for the stove . . .

He turned his chair slightly to look at his father's other great treasure, a two-tiered, five-plate jamb stove, which stood in a corner near the fireplace with the open end cunningly fitted into a hole in the wall, so that a servant could place fuel in it from another room without disturbing the master. Frau Mesner had hinted over and over again that the graceful stove, with its blue and white tiles depicting the story of Solomon's

Judgment, would be better suited to her dining room than to a place of business, but her husband refused even to consider relinquishing it.

"You do not realize, Elise," he said when she brought the subject up one morning at breakfast, "what a valuable piece that stove is. My grandfather ordered it specifically for the corner of the office back in 1734, and there it shall remain. Besides, the housemaids are sometimes careless; they might damage the tiles. Remember the tureen Lena broke? In any case, the iron box stove is adequate for the dining room, and more practical. That they cannot hurt."

Just like the clock, Philip thought as the last of the chimes died away; he is selfish as well as ruthless. Well, I am not his son for nothing, and when it comes to being ruthless—

"Philip!" The older man's sharp voice startled his son out of his reverie. "Be sure you confer with your mother about the clothing you will need for the trip. Hans, Herr Professor Lucknow is expecting you this evening punctually at eight o'clock, and every evening hereafter, including Sundays, for your lessons in English. Be sure you are on time.

"That is all for now—oh, on your way out send Ditmas in to me with the manifests for the *Damaskus*. Go now, and get on with your work. There is no time to be wasted." And with a dismissive wave he turned away from his sons and pulled a heavy ledger toward him.

It was after six o'clock when the brothers made their way through the warehouse behind the shipping office and stepped into the narrow alley that led to Friedrichstrasse.

"At least he's going to the Mariner's Club to a dinner tonight," Hans murmured, turning up the fur collar of his heavy winter coat against the wind from the river. "Perhaps we can have a meal without tears for a change. If he doesn't make Ella cry, he's sure to make Magda or Louisa leave the table."

6

"Hans, we must talk," Philip said impatiently. "Come up to my room as soon as you return from Herr Lucknow's."

"You sound as if you are thinking of rebelling, Philip," Hans said with a short laugh. "And a lot of good that will do you!"

"More than just thinking, Brother. I am making a plan, and you are part of it. Not a word, mind, to Mama, or to anyone else."

"What on earth? Does Father know? What plan? Do you dare—"

"Not now. There is no time. Don't worry if you are late tonight; I shall be awake. Open the door, for God's sake! I am turning to ice!"

Frau Mesner, a plump little woman in her late fifties endowed with a ready wit and a happy outlook on life, smiled as she listened to the chatter of her three daughters (uninhibited tonight in the absence of their father) as the evening meal progressed. If she noticed that Philip and Hans seemed occupied with their own thoughts, she gave no sign that she considered it anything but natural fatigue after a long working day.

The three girls were giggling over the awkwardness of the music master who came to the house three times a week to give Louisa and Ella violin lessons. Magda had no ear for music, but a sharp eye for a handsome man, and made a point of being on hand for Herr Fischer's arrival or departure.

"He's unable to take his eyes off you, Magda," Ella said teasingly. "That's why he stumbles over the doorsill."

"No," Louisa said quickly. "It's you he has his eye on, Ella. When you are playing he looks ready to eat you up."

"And how close he stands to her when he is showing her how to hold the bow!" Magda exclaimed. "I saw that this afternoon when you left the door open a bit—"

"Hans, some more apple cake? No? You, Philip?" Frau Mesner asked. "No? Then if we have finished we will let Lena clear the table. Hans, is it not time for you to leave for Herr Lucknow's?"

So, thought Philip, Father has told her. I wonder how she feels about it . . .

He did not have to wait long to find out: shortly after Hans left, the three girls took their needlework up close to the iron box stove in the corner of the dining room while Philip sat with his mother in the comfortably furnished but less well-heated parlor.

"I take it that you are aware of Father's plans for Hans and me," he said dryly, watching her adjust her woolen shawl and reach for the basket of knitting on the table beside her.

"Yes, my son, I have been told of them, and naturally I agree with your father. I am sure you will acquit yourself well, so that he will be proud of you, of both of you," she replied, keeping her eyes on her knitting needles.

"Has it occurred to you, Mama, that I might have been consulted, instead of being ordered? That I might not wish to go to America? That I might—as I do—wish to stay in Hamburg and marry Maria Schaefer?"

"Philip! You know your father frowns on any connection with the Schaefers! They are not of our class—"

"I do not know that being a shipping merchant is any more admirable than being a master cabinetmaker," Philip said quietly. "Have you seen the work Herr Schaefer and his men turn out? The chests, the armoires, the mantelpieces? The wealthiest families in Hamburg patronize his shop. But I suppose my father says that he is not our equal because Herr Schaefer works with his hands, and that therefore Maria is not good enough for me. And you, naturally, agree with him."

Frau Mesner sighed and, letting the needles rest on her lap, looked up at him for the first time.

"What you say is true, Philip, but nevertheless you must go, and you must go with good grace. You have always been headstrong, my son, and wanted things your way. You think of yourself first. I sometimes fear you are becoming a hard man."

"If that is so, Mama, it is my father who is to blame."

"Be that as it may, you must do his bidding in this. You must go—"

"Yes, I must go, Mama. I have no more choice than a babe in arms. But I warn you, that will change."

His mother shot him a quick, questioning look, but Philip was staring at the smoldering coals in the small grate, and said nothing further. She sighed once more, and after a moment resumed her knitting.

"Sorry to be so late," Hans said, breathless after his climb up the three flights of stairs to Philip's small bedroom. "After the lesson I stopped in at the Holders to see Elizabeth and tell her the news, but the whole family was there, so I couldn't."

"Good!" Philip exclaimed. "Don't tell anyone yet. You have a year to learn English, Brother, a year of grace, and who knows what may happen during that time? Now, listen: I am going to America as planned, but once there I shall disappear. No, don't interrupt! I shall embark on the *Ingrid* as Philip Mesner, but when the ship reaches New York I shall become someone else. I have not yet decided on a name, perhaps Paul Masters—a name with the same initials. There's time for that. Father's agent, Albert Pfeil, will never see me, nor will he have any means of tracing me. I shall make sure that does not happen.

"I have no intention of spending the next three or four years of my life working for that bad-tempered old man. When he was here last year he all but turned the place upside down, demanding this, demanding that, ordering us around as if we were slaves. You remember that, don't you? And how he reduced poor Ditmas to a quivering mass? Should Philip Mesner be subordinate to such a blowhard? No, no, and no! He's worse than Father. And all Father wants is to get me away from Maria, but he won't succeed there."

"But what will you do? How will you live?" Hans asked.

"Once in New York I shall lose myself, but not among the Germans—possibly among the Irish. I have not decided. When I get my bearings, I shall go into some business or other using whatever money Father gives me, plus what I have saved, as capital."

"You will be recognized—"

"No, Hans. That I will not. I'll grow a beard during the voyage, and take to wearing spectacles. It will be weeks, possibly months, before Father hears from Pfeil that I never arrived, and by that time I will have established my new identity.

"Now, this is where you come in: You may want to join me at some point—and I hope you do—but not until you have perfected your English. So we must keep in touch. When I write to Maria, who can be trusted to reveal nothing, I shall enclose letters for you. But I must have Elizabeth Holder's address, so that I can continue to write to you after I send for Maria, which I will do as soon as I can afford to marry. She and I have talked so many times about eloping that this will come as no surprise to her. I doubt that she will feel at all strange in America; her English is as good, if not better, than mine. You may remember that Herr Schaefer engaged both French and English tutors for her when she was younger, so that she could deal with the foreigners who came into his shop. Little did he know! See how I have thought it all out?"

"Yes, but—"

"No 'buts' now, Brother. It's late, and the fire has gone out. Go to bed; we'll talk more later on."

Hans nodded thoughtfully, then smiled ruefully.

10

"Can you imagine the storm that will break over our heads when Father realizes that you have deserted?"

"That will be the second storm, Hans," Philip said with a short laugh. "The first one will break almost immediately after I sail!"

Part
II

New York, 1830

John Ferguson locked the outer door of the offices of Ferguson and Lamb, Shipping Merchants, on South Street near Coenties Slip, and began to walk briskly through the November dusk north toward Maiden Lane. Life in New York had done remarkably little to alter the appearance of the young man who had stepped confidently off the *Ingrid* twenty years earlier. Only the touch of gray at the temples, hardly visible under the high crowned hat he wore to please Maria, and a slight fullness about the waistline indicated that he was no longer in his first youth. The erect bearing, the expertly trimmed beard, the alert expression in the dark eyes as he scanned the vessels tied up at the docks, proclaimed him to be a man of affairs, pleasant enough perhaps, but not readily approachable. Street urchins kept their distance from him.

He glanced up at the large window above a chandler's shop from which Albert Pfeil's sign had once hung, and grimaced at the shudder he was unable to repress. Will I never, he thought, be able to forget the fear I experienced during my first years here? Why can't I simply remember the exquisite relief I felt that day in 1812 when I received the letter from Hans saying Pfeil had died, and that Father had appointed the Wilkins Brothers as his agents? Only then did I stop taking roundabout routes to avoid passing that window for fear that Pfeil might look out and recognize me. Ah, well, better to think how fortunate I was that Father didn't send someone from the Hamburg office.

Pausing for a moment to study the line of tall-masted packets and cargo ships making ready to depart, he frowned and shook his head slightly before moving on. One of his own ships, the *Seagull,* should have docked three weeks ago, and since the fortunes of Ferguson and Lamb depended on her safe return he was understandably concerned. He knew, though, that the loading of nutmeg and other spices by the natives in Surinam was notoriously slow and in the past had delayed sailings by as much as a fortnight. It was in order to try to expedite matters that his partner, Otis Lamb, had decided to go on the run himself, in view of the considerable amount of money tied up in the shipment.

No, there is not yet reason to be concerned, not with my luck, Ferguson told himself, stepping aside to avoid a cartman guiding a wagon laden with bales of cotton shipped up from the South. And no reason to think my luck won't hold, none at all. He quickened his step, and whistling softly, turned his thoughts to how incredibly fortunate he'd been ever since he set foot in New York.

"Shipping is the only business I know," he had said to Maria shortly after her arrival from Hamburg in the spring of 1812, "so why venture into something I know nothing about? I had a bit of capital to invest—you know how I came by that—and Otis Lamb was just getting started and looking for a partner, a partner with money. It's working well and growing more profitable all the time."

"Was Otis Lamb not puzzled by your Irish name and your German accent?" Maria had asked. "How did you explain that away?"

"Easiest thing in the world, my love. I merely said that my father was an Irish banker who had met my mother while he was traveling in Germany, married her and carried her off to Ireland, where I was born. He died while I was still an infant in long clothes. Then my mother returned to her parents' home in Hamburg, where I was brought up. Is that not a credible story? Lamb must have swallowed it; he never dreamed of checking up on me."

"I always knew you had an inventive mind, Philip—I mean John—and now you must invent a way of teaching me more idiomatic English than I now speak. Oh, in that connection I must tell you that I do not believe Hans will ever join you. Your father changed his mind about sending him to Liverpool. Instead, Hans is to stay in Hamburg, which makes him happy because he wants to marry Elizabeth Holder. She's a timid little thing, and did not want to go to a strange country."

"Unlike you, my love," Ferguson said, putting his arms around her.

"Wait, Philip. I have more to tell you! When the letter came from the captain of the *Ingrid* saying you had been lost at sea your father was not seen for almost three weeks. We thought he must be ill—"

"Yes, Hans wrote that Father was not well, but he did not say what the sickness was. How has my mother been, do you know?"

"Yes," Maria replied. "Of course she mourned for you, but she did not break down, according to what Louisa told me. She cannot be very happy, I know, because shortly before I left Hamburg, maybe a week or ten days, your sister Ella ran off and married Herr Fischer, the music teacher."

"What!" Ferguson exclaimed. "Why would she do a thing like that? The featherbrain! And why didn't Hans tell me?"

17

"Perhaps he has too many other things on his mind. Louisa said your father depends on him more and more at the office. But tell me, John—see, I remembered!—were you not counting on Hans to work with you here?"

"It no longer matters whether Hans comes or not," he answered. "In fact, he might only complicate things if he did. Anyway, I do not need his help now. And I want no reminders of my life in Hamburg. My real life began when I first set foot in this city as John Ferguson."

"There is something else Louisa said, and it worries me," Maria went on. "Your father never for a moment believed that robbers had broken into his office. He sensed at once that you were the culprit, that you had taken the Ship's Clock and smashed his precious stove out of anger toward him. He was in such a rage, Hans told her, that he put a dreadful curse on you and on the clock, to be carried down to all your sons."

"Nonsense," Ferguson said brusquely when he saw Maria shudder. "Naturally he was angry and said whatever came into his head. But as for a curse—put it out of your mind, Maria."

Now, with a last lingering look at the river on his right, Ferguson turned into Maiden Lane, hurrying past a pig that was rooting in the refuse in front of Brower's grocery store, and wondering for perhaps the hundredth time if there weren't a better way of getting rid of garbage than throwing it out into the street for the ever-present pigs to eat. Once clear of the animal, he walked briskly on, pausing only to brush off a sad-looking mongrel that sniffed at his heels.

With the exception of a few private residences, Maiden Lane was a street of merchants who all lived above their shops. Ferguson strode past the carpenter's, the gunsmith's, the butcher's, and the shoemaker's, until he was opposite number 19. There he paused for a moment to admire the freshly painted shutters and the neat facade of the three-story wooden house, by far the finest residence on the block.

He had bought the house eight years earlier, at a good price when the previous owner was declared bankrupt. It was flanked by a hardware merchant's shop on one side and a piano warehouse on the other, both of them neat, clean enterprises whose owners allowed no accumulation of trash such as existed more or less permanently in front of the food merchants' shops farther down.

All very good, Ferguson thought as he crossed the street and mounted the three shallow steps to his front door. But nevertheless the time is coming for a move to a better neighborhood, a purely residential section. Not now, though: Maria is too near her time. Perhaps after the first of the year.

"Papa! What took you so long to cross the street? I watched you from the window and counted to twenty-seven while you stood in front of the shoemaker's. Dinner is ready—"

"Yes, indeed, little one, you are right to scold me for holding up your dinner," he said, smiling down at his favorite child, a dainty little girl, who tugged at his sleeve. "But I cannot go to dinner with my hat and coat on, now can I, Annetta? Where is your Mama?"

"Upstairs, Papa. Ellen has taken a tray up to her. Is Mama sick?"

Before she finished speaking, Ferguson was halfway up the steep flight of stairs, and a moment later he was leaning over the pale-faced woman who lay in the high double bed.

"The baby is coming, John," she said softly. "Send to Dr. Bogert—be quick—oh—"

He held her hand until the pain subsided and then dashed down the stairs again, shouting for his children.

"Robert! Robert! Run for Dr. Bogert! Go at once! James, go for Mrs. Page—the red house on the corner of Liberty Street. Hurry! Hurry! Ellen, where the devil are you? Oh, there—tell Emma to heat some water. Annetta, stay out of the way . . ."

★　★　★

"I shall name him Paul, Maria," Ferguson said the next morning as he stood watching the infant sleep in the cradle he had made for his firstborn child. "I was going to take that name myself once, remember?"

"It's your turn, John," Maria said with a tired smile. "I name the girls and you name the boys, so Paul he shall be, a genuine Paul."

"He is perfect, isn't he?" her husband asked anxiously. "Has all his toes and fingers, has he? He is so wrapped up I cannot tell."

"That he is, Mr. Ferguson," the nurse said as she bustled into the room carrying a tray. "A perfect little man he is, but your lady must rest now. 'Twas a very difficult birth."

"Yes, yes, of course, Mrs. Page," he answered impatiently. "I'm on my way to the office. Try to sleep, my love. Tonight I'll look in on you."

Thank God it's over, he thought as he strode rapidly toward South Street. Maria is safe, and my son is safe; now if only there is news of Lamb and the *Seagull*. I'll give them another week, and then . . .

Before the week was out, however, the news was in: The *Letitia W.*, a ship owned by Harmon and Company, limped into port carrying four survivors of the *Seagull*, which had broken up in a storm off Hatteras. The cargo from Surinam, the rest of the crew, and Otis Lamb had all gone down with the ship.

Part
III

Ellen

When the *Seagull* sank in the fall of 1830 my father went through what he later referred to as the doldrums of his life. He and Otis Lamb had not only borrowed heavily to finance the voyage, but they had also chosen to forego any maritime insurance, with the result that Ferguson and Lamb failed, leaving my father deeply in debt.

"Insurance would have been an additional expense," he explained to my brother Robert, who at seventeen had left school when the *Seagull* went down and started to work at the City National Bank, and rather prided himself on his knowledge of finance. "We reasoned that since Lamb was going along there would be little danger of skullduggery or chicanery on the part of the crew. He had a way with the men, Lamb did. But now—good God! Everything is gone! Everything! Ferguson and Lamb is bankrupt, and I do not see any way of paying my creditors! I shall end up in the debtors' prison—I shall go mad!"

Indeed, the worry about finances, plus his deep concern for my mother, who had been dangerously ill with childbed fever after Paul's birth, nearly did drive him mad, and his bad temper and perpetual frown caused us to keep out of his way as much as possible. Even little Annetta, his favorite, would hide when she heard him approaching. Only to my mother did he speak softly; to the rest of us he barked out commands, or raised his voice to complain. Inevitably an atmosphere of fear and gloom soon pervaded 19 Maiden Lane, settling down over us like a dark cloud, and showing no sign of lifting.

Robert's meager salary was the only money coming in, and in order to economize, Papa had let Emma, the maid, go. I was afraid he'd dismiss Mrs. Boggs, the cook, too, but he didn't. Fortunately for us he also kept Mrs. Page on to take care of Mama. I say fortunately because it was the nurse who finally came to our rescue.

Several times during her extended stay at 19 Maiden Lane Mrs. Page had expressed amazement at Papa's handiwork. She admired the cradle, of course, but besides that she had noted and exclaimed over other things: the mechanical toys with which Annetta still played, Mama's reversible embroidery frame, the intricately carved trivets for hot pots and dishes, and the retractable ladder for the trapdoor to the attic, all beautifully put together and given a professional finish.

"You have the mind of an inventor, Mr. Ferguson," she said, nodding at the little two-tiered wooden box that held buttons as she stitched away on a pair of suspenders she was making for her husband. "Why don't you try your hand at designing suspenders, sir? You cannot buy them anyplace, and the Lord knows men need them to hold up their trousers. This is but a poor cloth thing I am making, and will not last, but could you not create a pair out of leather, with fancy clasps and all? There would indeed be a market for them."

At first her suggestion did not appeal to him. I believe he

thought making a contraption to hold up men's trousers would be beneath him. In the end he surprised us, though.

"I do not wish to be disturbed," he said one morning as he rose from the breakfast table. Without further explanation he left the dining room and locked himself in the small room behind the parlor, which he called his "home office." In one corner his tools hung in a neat row above the small workbench he had constructed himself, while a flattop desk and its chair occupied the opposite wall. Papa's greatest treasure, the Ship's Clock, stood in the exact center of the desk, and when we were little he would sometimes invite us in at noon on a Sunday to watch the little figures march across the deck when the clock struck. The door to that room was always kept locked, and sometimes, when Papa was not at home, we would press our ears against it to hear the chimes, and then walk our fingers back and forth as we had seen the tiny seamen do. But that was long ago.

It was in his "home office" that my father spent most of his time that dreary winter of 1830-31, and we saw little of him except at meals. It was not a good winter for me. Early in January, when Mrs. Page left to go on another case after Mama was up and about, and when Papa saw how easily she tired, he made me give up the classes I had been attending at Miss Geraldine Tremayne's house.

"You are young and strong, Ellen," he said firmly. "You can easily take care of the few things that need attention in this little house. Anyone could do it. Now will you see to the washing at once. I have no clean shirts."

I was frightened by the gruffness in his voice when he issued that last command, but when I saw how worried he looked, and thought of how ill Mama had been, I knew I had to be of as much help as possible. I had been rather bored with my lessons in French and music, but after a few days of household chores I would gladly have gone back to them.

How Emma managed to do all the sweeping, scrubbing, and polishing, to say nothing of attending to the piles of laundry, and still remain cheerful, I will never know. But at least she was paid for her work, while I had nothing to show for my labors at the end of the month but rough, chapped hands, broken fingernails, and a sour disposition. I began to feel like a drudge, and whenever I caught sight of myself in Mama's looking glass I knew that I looked like one. My hair, which I was too tired to brush the prescribed hundred strokes at night, looked unkempt; my complexion was sallow, and my eyes were bloodshot, probably from the lye I had to use in the scrub water. And I neither looked nor felt clean.

No one, not even Mama, seemed to notice either my drab appearance or my misery until one bitterly cold day late in February, when I burst into tears and put my head down on the scrubbed surface of the kitchen table. Mrs. Boggs, ordinarily a complacent, easygoing woman, had been cranky all morning, muttering to herself that if she wasn't paid at the end of the month she would have to leave.

"And where would I go?" she moaned. "It's all very well for you, Missy. Your Papa will see that you have a roof over your head, but would he lift a finger if I was out in the streets with naught but the clothes on my back? Ow, ow, now look—"

The pot of soup she'd been stirring suddenly boiled over, and she hastily removed it from the stove. In her exasperation she set it down on the table with such a thump that the hot liquid spilled, not only on the towels I was folding, but on my work-roughened hands as well.

I was still sobbing so uncontrollably, more in despair than in pain, that when Mama appeared in the kitchen and asked what the matter was I could not speak. Even after she treated my burns with her salves and ointments, and sat with her arms around me, I continued to cry.

"There, there, Liebchen," she crooned, stroking my hair.

"It will soon be better. There won't even be a scar, not the tiniest one; you'll see. Don't cry, little one—but you are no longer a little one, you're a grown girl now, fourteen years old. And you've been a good girl, Ellen. All these weeks I've been sick I never realized how much hard work you were doing, and how hard it was on your poor hands. I will make some changes . . ."

What changes, I wondered. She could not do the housework, Mrs. Boggs wouldn't do it, and where was the money coming from for another Emma? I said nothing, however, and in a little while Mama began to hum one of the old German lullabies she loved. I was almost asleep when the door flew open and Papa burst into the room, holding what appeared to be two black leather straps and a puzzling array of metal clips.

"I have made it, Maria," he said happily. "You see before you the source of our future wealth!"

He almost danced across the room to us, at the same time speaking rapidly about going to Washington to have his invention patented.

"There has never been anything like it, Maria. Think how the firemen will go for it! It will sell like hot cakes. God bless Mrs. Page!"

While the suspender business did not make us wealthy overnight, it did allow us, after a while, to live comfortably. Papa traveled to Washington, an arduous trip by stage and packet ship in those days, and returned with the news that he had obtained the patent application he wanted under the name of Ferguson's Patented Suspenders.

He was a new man, cheerful, confident, and far kinder than he had been. Immediately upon his return he set to work, and for a time the household was in an uproar. He converted the front room, Mama's parlor, into a shop and set up his factory in the basement, since his "home office" was totally inadequate. His first customers were, as he had predicted, the firemen, and it was through my brother James that he obtained their patronage.

Ever since he was eight or nine years old, Jay, like so many other boys in the neighborhood, had been a follower of fire engines. These young "runners," as they were called, ran alongside the engines as they raced through the crowded streets of lower New York, hoping for a chance to help put out a fire. When the alarm sounded, either by the ringing of church bells or by a signal from the fire wardens stationed in the wooden watchtowers, the firemen, all volunteers, would drop what they were doing and man the engines, some of which were hand drawn and others pulled by horses. Their equipment, consisting as it did of hand-pumped engines, leather buckets, and canvas hoses, was seldom adequate, and the men were often unable to contain the conflagrations that so frequently plagued our city. Up until the time fireplugs, or hydrants, as they were later called, were installed on various corners, water had to be drawn from the city wells or one of the rivers. In many cases, though, the fireplugs were so far away from the blaze that the men were reduced to passing the water-filled leather buckets hand over hand, never a satisfactory arrangement.

Jay was well known at the house of Engine Number 13 at the foot of Maiden Lane near the fish market, and it wasn't long before the firemen of that company were wearing bright yellow suspenders sporting a leather clasp in the shape of an eagle's widespread wings atop the number thirteen. A short time later engine companies from other parts of the city were demanding custom-made suspenders with specific insignias on the clasps—a lion's head, a star, a lantern, or suchlike. By the end of a year, when Papa was designing and producing not only suspenders but also brassards for caps and helmets, he found it necessary to train two apprentices, and at that point Mama rebelled.

"This is no longer my house, John," she said one night at the dinner table. "It is a place of business, and we are living in a state of constant noise and confusion. Could you not move your factory and your store someplace else? Or move your family to a proper residence? I should like very much to have my parlor to myself once more."

It was so unusual for Mama to complain about anything at all that Papa stared at her in surprise. After a moment or two, though, he smiled.

"I completely forgot," he said. "It went right out of my mind when the *Seagull* was lost. Just before that happened I had been giving some thought to moving to a better neighborhood. Yes, Maria, now I can see my way clear to finding you a proper house!"

Nothing happened immediately, but in the spring of 1832 he rented 233 Broadway for us, an elegant four-story house next door to the mansion owned by Mr. Philip Hone, a former mayor of New York. Our new home was neither as large nor as showy as Mr. Hone's, but it had its own air of elegance. From the wrought iron railings on the low stoop to the dormer windows projecting from the steeply slanted slate roof, nothing was out of line or character. The design on the stone lintels over the windows on the second and third floors duplicated the pattern of leaves carved above the front door, and was repeated again in the frieze that ran along the top of the bow window in the parlor. But best of all, we were able to do away with candles and oil lamps; 233 was one of the few houses in the city to have gaslight at that time.

Papa kept the house in Maiden Lane as his workplace, and as the business grew with orders from the police, the city militia, and various clubs, he added so many to his staff of workers that in a short time every room in our old house was given over to the production of suspenders, belts, caps, and emblems of all sorts.

Mama was delighted with her new home, and Papa gave her

enough money to furnish it as she liked. I don't know how many times I heard her say how wonderful it was to have a proper parlor again. If Papa heard her, he would smile tolerantly and say that what he liked best about the house was that from his window he saw only the *occasional* pig on Broadway. Things were going well for him then, and we were all grateful that he was more cheerful than he'd been since the loss of the *Seagull*. In spite of the improved atmosphere, though, I could not erase from my mind the memory of the bad-tempered man he had been. How, I asked myself, is it possible for a person to change so completely? Or is he really two men, a dark one in times of adversity and a bright one when times are prosperous? Perhaps, I thought, that is perfectly normal, and I should give him the benefit of the doubt. But still, I wondered.

Our lives were settling down into a pattern of sorts: Robert was happy working at the City National Bank, Jay was enrolled at Columbia College, Annetta was sent to Trinity, the famous Episcopalian school, and little Paul continued to thrive. Mama arranged for me to attend a private academy on Varick Street, across from St. John's Park, one of the more fashionable neighborhoods at that time. The school was run by Miss Augustina Atwell and her sister, Miss Georgina, of the once socially prominent Atwell family. Old Mr. Atwell it was said, had taken to his bed after gambling away a considerable fortune, leaving his daughters no alternative but to take in pupils in order to make ends meet. On occasion we would hear the loud ringing of a bell (it sounded like a dinner gong) from the floor above our classroom, and then Miss Augustina would excuse herself for a few minutes, presumably to attend to the needs of the old gentleman.

In the ballroom at the rear of the mansion, where once the elite of New York had been entertained, Miss Georgina taught us to dance. Miss Augustina thumped away at the pianoforte while we practiced the steps of the waltz, the polka, the cotillion, or the quadrille under her sister's direction.

"Hold your head erect, Ellen!" she would cry out. "You are *not*, I repeat, *not* to look at your feet. Grace, your elbows! Pull them in. Lighter on your feet, Amanda; you are not marching, you are dancing! Now, sit down all of you, while I demonstrate."

When we had arranged ourselves on the fragile gold and white chairs against the wall she would go through the steps for us, and then conclude the day's lesson with a lecture on how to comport ourselves on the dance floor. Miss Augustina's lectures on history and art (which she read from various books piled on her desk) did not hold our interest, but Miss Georgina had our undivided attention when she spoke to us in the ballroom. No one of us wanted to risk a gaffe in public if and when we were invited to a ball.

I thoroughly enjoyed the dancing, but what I liked best about the academy was the opportunity it afforded me to associate with girls my own age, two of whom became lifelong friends. Bettina Lawrence was a lovely slender brunette, whose dark eyes enslaved my brother Robert the first time she appeared at our dinner table. Margit van Eyck, her Dutch ancestry apparent in her cornflower blue eyes and flaxen hair, was equally attractive, and the more vivacious of the two.

I never felt that I could compete with either one of them as far as looks were concerned, but when I said as much to my mother she consoled me by saying that my features were more regular than Bettina's and my complexion far superior to Margit's. I didn't quite believe her, but she may have known what she was talking about, for I have known two men who found me beautiful—but that was later, after the epidemic.

In the late spring of 1832 we heard the first reports of the cholera in the western hemisphere. The disease, which began in Asia and spread throughout Europe, surfaced in Quebec in May, and by the end of June several cases had appeared in New York.

There was no Fourth of July celebration that year; either the board of health or some other authority canceled the usual parade and all other activities involving large gatherings. In spite of these precautions, however, several new cases were reported that very day. We were not allowed out of doors, and when Papa and Robert left for work the day after the quiet Fourth, Mama watched them from the bow window with tears streaming down her face. She looked so miserable that I was almost relieved when she turned sharply on Jay, who was grumbling about being housebound.

"I'm seventeen years old, Mama," he protested, "and you're treating me like a lad of seven."

"You will do as I say, Jay," she said firmly, "and right now I say you are to put up those extra shelves Anna has been wanting in the pantry. The lumber is in the basement."

Jay slouched out of the room, muttering something I could not hear. I wonder, now, if Mama wasn't glad of an excuse to keep him in the house, under her eye; she'd hinted several times that she was not happy about his late nights, and I'm sure she was worried about the company he was keeping. When we were younger Jay and I had no secrets from each other; we were almost exactly a year apart in age, and more or less grew up together. But lately, as was only natural, our interests had changed, and we'd grown apart. In a way, I could understand Mama's concern. We had no idea what Jay did when he went out at night, nor did we know who his friends were, since he never brought any of them home.

The prospect of weeks, perhaps months, spent indoors was anything but appealing, and I was greatly relieved when Mr. Hone, our good neighbor, stopped in on the evening of July seventh to tell us he was taking his family to the seashore for the rest of the summer. He advised us to leave the city as soon as possible; people, he said, were fleeing by the hundreds, and we would be wise to follow suit.

At first Papa refused to consider such a suggestion, but when

he realized how worried and frightened Mama was he capitu-
lated and rented a house for us in Rockaway, a block away
from the ocean. He and Robert would remain in the city, he
said, and Mama was not to worry about them. They would
travel down to the shore on weekends so that she could check
up on them.

If it had not been for the ominous daily reports of the board
of health of the continuing escalation of the number of deaths
from the cholera, our first summer out of New York would
have been an unqualified success. I loved the hours we spent
at the water's edge, even though we could do little more than
wet our feet. Although Mama had provided us all with bathing
dress we were forbidden to venture into the breakers (even
Jay) unless Papa was there. That made the weekends something very special. What a change from other summers we had
known! And the nights! Instead of lying awake in humid,
airless rooms we went to sleep readily, with breezes from the
ocean often making blankets a necessity—a far cry from the
hot sultriness of the city. Of course it had to end; toward the
latter part of August the epidemic was declared over, and we
returned, somewhat reluctantly, to the Broadway house.

"One more year, Liebchen," Mama said one morning early in
September. "Only one more year must you go to the Misses
Atwell, then we shall see."
    "And you, James," Papa said sternly, "you must apply your-
self more seriously to your studies than you did last year. No
more going out at night—"
    "Not even Friday or Saturday?" Jay expostulated.
    "No, not at all," Papa replied, and picked up his newspaper
as a sign that the conversation was over.
    Mama had sat quietly at her end of the breakfast table during
this exchange, but I knew that it was she who had prompted
Papa to speak to Jay.

33

I had not meant to eavesdrop, but that's what it amounted to. After dinner the night before I had gone up to the small sewing room to finish whipping some edging onto a collar I thought too plain, and had almost finished when I heard my parents come upstairs. The master bedroom was directly across the hall from where I sat, but neither of them glanced in my direction, nor did they close the door before Mama began to speak.

"There were two boys on the other side of Broadway, John," she said. "They were waiting for him. Rough-looking boys, ill clad, with their shirttails hanging out. And as soon as James joined them they all three raced away across the park, laughing and shouting, as if they were running to a fire."

"I do not like it, Maria," Papa said brusquely, "and I shall put a stop to it."

At that point the door was closed and I heard no more. I wasn't sure how angry Papa was, but I thought I ought to warn Jay to be on his guard.

James

Thanks to Ellen's warning I was not altogether unprepared for my father's injunction. Although I was desolated for a reason that I will reveal later, I was almost relieved that I had a genuine excuse for terminating my association with Randy O'Dair and Bobby Sweeney. Those two were in no way evil or wicked companions, but they had too much time on their hands plus a propensity for attracting trouble, and not much common sense.

I had known them several years earlier during that period of my life when I was spending most of my free time at the firehouse of Engine Number 13. Like me, they haunted the place, and when an alarm sounded the three of us would race along beside the firewagons, filled with excitement and dreams of glory. In time I developed other interests, but O'Dair and Sweeney went on to become bona fide members of the company and privileged to wear Ferguson's Patented Suspenders with the special insignia.

I hadn't seen much of them since I started college, but one evening in the spring of 1832 I ran into them when I went down to Whitehall Street to watch a fire. They spotted me, and once the fire was under control urged me to accompany them to a meeting of the Kerryonians, a street gang made up solely of Irishmen.

"Yer Irish, aintcha, Ferguson?" Sweeney asked. "With that name you gotta be. And it's yer patriotic dooty to stand up for yer nationality!"

"That it is," O'Dair chimed in. "Down with Blighty! Come on! We'll take you to Rosanna's and make you a member."

I had no wish to become a member of the Kerryonians, or of any of the other gangs that roamed the streets fighting, thieving, even killing, and said so.

"Aw, we're not a fightin' gang like the Plug Uglies an' the Dead Rabbits, Jamie," Sweeney protested. "We just think on hatin' the English; we meet, and talk, have a few drinks—it's a grand time we have. Come on, boyo, see for yourself."

I was curious enough to go with them, but it wasn't long before I was wishing I'd kept a rein on my curiosity. On Center Street, just below Anthony, we stopped in front of a rundown grocery store, which seemed to have a few wilted vegetables as its only stock. My companions smiled at my puzzled expression, and then led me through the empty shop to a door in the rear. O'Dair knocked, a special rat-rat-tat, and almost immediately I heard a bolt slide back and chains being undone. The door opened slowly, but only a crack.

"It's us, Kev," O'Dair said, "O'Dair and Sweeney an' a new member. Open up!"

That's when I should have turned and fled.

Sweeney pushed me ahead of him into a room so dimly lighted that at first I could see nothing. My foot slipped on something wet on the floor, and I almost went headlong. Candles were the only source of illumination, and when my eyes adjusted to the dim light I could see five or six men sitting at a round table in the middle of the room and three others leaning against a bar that took up most of the wall behind them. They showed little interest in our arrival, and after a cursory inspection of the "new member" returned to the conversation the unbolting of the door had interrupted. "Conversation" is hardly the right word; the shouts and obscenities directed against England (and anything connected with the English people), and punctuated by much table thumping and foot stamping, bore no resemblance to that gentle art.

Sweeney propelled me over to the bar, behind which an enormously fat woman with a head of greasy black hair officiated.

"Drinks, Rosie," he shouted, slapping a few coins on the counter. "For us, and my friend here."

While the woman was pouring a few ounces of a dark brown liquid into three battered tin cups he turned to me, smiling.

"Cheapest booze in the city, Rosie has," he said. "Ain't that right, O'Dair?"

"Right, mate. Come on, drink up, Jamie, and I'll stand the next round," O'Dair replied.

One mouthful of that vile spiritous liquor was enough to set my entire insides on fire; I choked, gagged, and coughed to such an extent that the rest of the company paused in their damning of the Union Jack to laugh at my discomfiture. When I regained my composure and ventured a second (small) sip of the brew, they applauded and then forgot about me. O'Dair and Sweeney seemed to have forgotten about me as well; they moved over to join the group at the table, leaving me standing at the bar, uncertain of my next move.

I wanted desperately to leave the dirty, foul-smelling room, but I was afraid an abrupt departure would be taken as an insult, and I had a healthy respect for the temper of an insulted

Irishman. So, I pretended to show an interest in my surroundings while I brought the tin cup to my lips (only pretending to drink) from time to time. When I saw O'Dair approach the bar for another drink I surreptitiously spilled what remained in my cup on the already sodden floor, and stood well back in the shadows, hoping he'd not remember that I was there at all.

Luck was with me: Two of the burlier men rose from the table, and lurched rather than walked up to the bar, blocking any view O'Dair might have had of me. A third man followed them, and either he was far gone in drink or else he honestly slipped on one of the wet boards—maybe where I'd spilled my liquor. He grabbed hold of the big fellow nearest him for support, and the two of them went down with such a thunderous crash that I thought they must be dead.

In the confusion that followed I looked around for a means of escape; I didn't think I could get to the door by which we had entered, let alone deal with the chains and bolts on it, so I turned my attention to the area behind the bar. At that moment someone held one of the candles up, high above the heads of those crowding around the two on the floor, and by its light I could see a shabby curtain hanging over what looked like a doorway to a room behind the one we were in.

No one paid any attention to me when I went down on my hands and knees and crawled behind the bar. I slipped, or rather slithered, behind fat Rosanna, and made for the curtain, which I pulled aside at the bottom just far enough to allow me to pass through the opening into complete darkness. I felt my way along the wall on my right, tripped over a chair or stool, and continued on until my fingers came into contact with the closed shutters of a window.

Opening the shutters was no problem—they were like the ones we'd had in the Maiden Lane house—but the window itself either had a special lock on it, or else was permanently sealed up. Strain as I might, I could not raise the sash, and in the end could think of naught else to do but to smash the glass with my heavy boot. I wasted no time wondering if the break-age had been heard in the other room but climbed out into the night as fast as I could.

Terrified of pursuit, I ran without stopping until I reached the familiar docks on South Street. After resting in a dark doorway until my heart stopped pounding I made my way homeward, careful to stay on streets where people were still abroad until I reached Broadway. A few minutes later I was in front of my own house, and as I looked through the lace curtains in the bow window I was surprised to see that the gas jets were lighted and that a whist game was in progress. So much had happened to me that I thought it must be long after midnight . . .

I let myself in quietly and stood in the vestibule for a moment before creeping up the stairs. Ellen looked up from the book she was reading and gasped at my disheveled appearance, as I passed her bedroom door, but I knew she wouldn't give me away.

On my way home from college one day the following week I saw O'Dair and Sweeney approaching on the opposite side of the street, and quickly stepped into a dry goods store until they passed on. I was in no hurry to find out what their reaction to my desertion of them might be. The next day, however, they caught up with me as I emerged from my last class, and to my surprise congratulated me right roundly on being smart enough to leave Rosanna's when I did.

It seems that shortly after I made my escape the police broke down the door between the shop and the back room, causing the drinkers to flee through the rear—apparently there was a back door I had not seen in the darkness—leaving the two who had fallen on the floor to deal with the law.

"You musta heard them comin', eh, Jamie?" Sweeney said admiringly. "Sharp ears you got, boyo."

"What brought the police there?" I asked.

"Oh, we heard they was lookin' for Wild Willie Wogg, him that robbed a silversmith on Maiden Lane," O'Dair replied. "He wasn't there that night, though."

"But you said—" I began.

"It's safe to go back there now," Sweeney interrupted. "Rosie has the place cleaned up. She was that mad about a winder that got broken, though, so we took up a collection. How's about meetin' us there tomorrer night, Jamie?"

"No, I can't," I said firmly. "I have something else on for tomorrow night."

"Ah, come off it, Jamie," O'Dair said sullenly. "Yer a member now. Besides, you owe us for a round of drinks—"

"Here," I said, taking a half dollar from my pocket, "take this, and have your drinks. I'll see if I can get away early enough to meet you."

That seemed to satisfy them, at least for the time being, but I knew they'd be back. I also knew that I'd better have a damn good excuse ready when they intercepted me again; they were not the type to give up easily. For the next several weeks, however, I saw nothing of them, and then, because of the epidemic, we went to Rockaway for the summer.

When we returned to the city at the end of August I kept a wary eye out for the two Kerryonians, but there was no sign of them. Thinking that they might have been victims of the cholera, I went down to 9 Canal Street, where Mr. S. Ming, publisher of the daily *Health Reporter*, had his office. When I explained that I feared two of my friends had succumbed to the disease while I was out of the city, I was permitted to see copies of the daily lists of deaths. I could find no mention of either Sweeney or O'Dair on any of them, but Mr. Ming told me that the lists were far from complete.

"There were probably plenty that we missed, lad," he said in a sorrowful tone. "Those that didn't want it known that the cholera had struck their family buried their dead secretly, carrying them out by night. And there were tales of bodies tossed in the river, but who knows? Maybe your friends escaped."

I had no idea where O'Dair and Sweeney lived, but after thanking Mr. Ming for his time I walked over to Center Street to have a look at Rosanna's shop in the daytime, only to find that it had burned to the ground sometime during the summer. That was the end of the Kerryonians, or so I thought at the time.

I turned away from the charred ruin, and walked without purpose (classes had not yet begun at Columbia, so I had time on my hands) until I came to the Park Theater, an impressive building almost directly across City Hall Park from our house on Broadway. I paused to examine a billboard announcing that *The School for Scandal,* featuring Miss Fanny Kemble, would open shortly. Tickets would go on sale early in September. Suddenly I was aware that a carriage had drawn up in front of the theater, and that a crowd had gathered to watch its occupants descend.

"It's her!" exclaimed a young dandy, pushing me out of his way.

"Who? Who is it?" I asked a painted woman with a feather boa draped over her shoulders. "Is that—"

"Yes, indeed, dearie," she answered. "That's Miss Fanny herself. Come for rehearsal, no doubt. Sweet, ain't she?"

More than sweet, I thought, watching the elaborately dressed, smiling young woman make her way across the pavement. She nodded graciously to the gathering crowd, paused to sign her name to a piece of paper thrust at her by an eager youth, and after waving a small, white-gloved hand to her admirers, turned to enter the theater. Since the billboard I had been looking at was fairly close to the main door, the vision of loveliness passed within a couple of feet of where I was standing. I bowed from the waist, and bid her good day, but when I straightened up she'd disappeared into the lobby of the theater.

41

Embarrassed by the amused glances of some of the bystand-ers, I stood still, wondering how best to make a dignified exit. I don't know what I would have done if one of my classmates, Dan Jennings, had not tapped me on the shoulder and dragged me off to have lunch with him.

"You couldn't have come along at a better time, Dan," I said as we headed toward a nearby coffee house. "I didn't know which way to turn. What were you doing there, any-way?"

"I was on my way back from the bookstore when I saw the carriage draw up, and stopped to watch," he answered. "Is she real, do you think? I couldn't get close enough to see whether it was all paint and powder."

Obviously Jennings took a more skeptical view of beauty than I did, but nevertheless he was a good fellow.

From then on, until school reopened, I haunted the Park Theater, hoping for a glimpse of the dazzling star. I became a regular stage door Johnnie, and quickly struck up acquaintance with two other lovesick youths, both of whom had been promised jobs as stagehands "should any openings occur." They were nice-looking lads, and might even have made handsome appearances if they'd paid attention to their cloth-ing. I gathered they were short, extremely short of money, for they wore no jackets even on a cool evening, and let their shirttails hang out to cover worn parts of their trousers. But they were good company, pleasant, happy-go-lucky fellows, and as badly smitten as I was with the leading lady.

I liked them well enough, but when Dan Jennings began to turn up at the stage door I preferred passing the time with him.

"I really don't know what I'm doing here, Jay," he said one night as we waited for the actress to appear, "except that after I saw the play I couldn't get Fanny Kemble out of my mind." Perhaps he wasn't so skeptical after all.

Before I could comment the stage door opened and a mo-ment later the object of our admiration was whisked through the crowd on the arm of a tall gentleman in evening dress and handed into a waiting carriage. I thought she smiled at me, or at least in my direction.

I had just decided to purchase a nosegay to present to Miss Kemble after one of the performances when Papa put an end to my evening excursions. For a while I thought I might die of a broken heart, but surprisingly enough, I made a speedy recovery. Evidently Jennings did, too, because it wasn't long before he was madly in love with Miss Laura Grayson, whom he later married.

When, a few years later, I read that Miss Kemble had married Pierce Butler, a planter, and had gone to live in the South, I could hardly remember what she looked like. So much for youthful vows of undying love . . .

Robert

Jay didn't know I had seen the picture of Miss Fanny Kemble under his pile of white shirts, and I never told him. I was in a hurry to find a clean one of my own—Miss Bettina Lawrence was expected for dinner that night—and had opened his drawer by mistake. Poor kid, I thought, there's little hope for you in that quarter. He couldn't have been too badly smitten with the actress, though, because a short time later I saw that the picture had been torn in half and thrown into the trash basket.

Although we were separated in age by only two years, and had shared a bedroom ever since I could remember, Jay and I had never been particularly close. A matter of interest, I suppose; he was still running after fire engines when I had to leave school and go to work after Papa's shipping business failed. In 1832 he was still a schoolboy, and a rather immature one at that, without any particular goal in mind.

I, on the other hand, had known for years what I wanted to

do with my life: I intended to make a great deal of money, using my head rather than my hands, invest it carefully, letting money make more money for me, and then marry Bettina Lawrence. I'd already bought a few shares of stock here and there, based on tips from a broker who banked with us. Railroads were the thing to be in, he told me, and since I knew about the success of the Boston to Albany line, I invested whatever I could spare from my salary—first in the Erie Railroad, which proposed to follow the southern border of New York State and extend to Lake Erie just south of Buffalo. My second choice was the Hudson River Railroad, which ran from New York only to Poughkeepsie, but planned to continue on to Albany. I didn't see how I could lose.

I would retire, I thought, at the age of forty, and devote myself to comfortable living, dividing my time between a mansion in Manhattan and an estate in the country. And, of course, I would travel; I wanted to see other financial centers besides New York, and I also wanted to visit the city of Hamburg, where my parents had lived. My father was reticent about his early life, and rarely spoke of it, leading me to wonder whether there was something in his ancestry of which he was ashamed.

He had apparently severed all connections to whatever family he'd had in Germany; we were told only that he'd been born in Ireland, and was still in his infancy when his father died, after which he and his mother returned to her native Hamburg. Apparently he grew up there, but no mention was ever made of aunts, uncles, or other relatives. We learned early not to ask questions . . .

The only memento of his early life was the Ship's Clock, which now stood on the mantel in the parlor. Papa said his grandfather had willed it to him, and that it would eventually come to me, the oldest son. When, however, I asked him which grandfather it was, the German one or the Irish one, he pretended not to hear me. He could do that with authority.

Over the years he'd lost all trace of a German accent, and spoke the English of an educated New Yorker. He would permit no German to be spoken in our household, and frowned whenever my mother, in a moment of emotion, lapsed into the language of her youth. Her English was technically correct, but it would not have taken a speech expert to discern that it was not her mother tongue.

A knowledge of German might have been helpful to me; it would be an asset, I thought, if I ever became involved in international banking. That was a possibility, but I liked what I was doing at the City National Bank; I liked the aura of wealth that permeated the building; I liked the signs of prosperity in the dress and appearance of the officers; I liked the expensively furnished rooms, the Persian rugs, and the heavy mahogany furniture, and I clung to the dream of one day sitting in the high-backed chair in the president's corner office. I did not want anything to do with the suspender business on Maiden Lane, even though Papa had built it up into a highly profitable enterprise. He frequently said that he hoped Jay and I would take it over one day, but I think he knew that as far as I was concerned my brother could have it all.

He was talking about how well the company was doing one raw Sunday afternoon in March of 1833 when we were both in the parlor. I was simply killing time until the earliest moment I could decently leave to appear at the Lawrence home, to which I had been bid for supper, and he was waiting for Mama to come down and send for coffee and cake. He was in the middle of a lecture on the importance of patents when the doorbell sounded. He looked annoyed, and motioned impatiently that I should see to it.

"Excuse me, sir," said the gentleman who stood on the doorstep, "but is this the residence of Mr. John Ferguson? And if so, would you tell him that Mr. Timothy Ferguson would like a word with him?"

I was too startled to do anything but nod stupidly and hold

the inner door for him while the thought flashed through my mind that he looked somewhat like my father, except that his expression was more kindly. In the hall he handed me his high hat and frock coat, and stood waiting politely. I introduced myself, and then led the way into the parlor. Papa rose from his chair as we entered the room and stared hard at our visitor, who smiled and shook his head slightly.

"I beg your pardon, sir, for this intrusion," he said. "My name is Timothy Ferguson, and I—are you all right, sir?"

The color had drained from my father's face, and he seemed to sway to one side. In a second or two, however, he regained control of himself.

"Quite all right, thank you. A sudden stab of sciatica, with which I am troubled occasionally. Please be seated. Now, how can I be of service to you?"

"Now that I have seen you, Mr. Ferguson," our guest answered, "I do not believe you can." He had a pleasant voice and spoke well, but his accent puzzled me. I knew it was not German—possibly Irish? But no, I was familiar enough with that brogue.

"Let me explain," he went on. "I am trying to locate my brother, John, who disappeared more than twenty years ago. I have reason to believe that he may have settled in New York, and have been checking all the Fergusons I can find. Although you resemble him to some degree, it is obvious to me that you are not he. John had deep blue eyes, not your dark brown ones. Pray excuse the intrusion."

"No need for apologies, my dear sir." Papa responded in such measured tones that I felt he was monitoring his speech. "Looking for a lost brother is certainly an admirable undertaking."

"I doubt that John would agree with you there, sir, were I to find him. You see, I have a score to settle with him; he did me out of my inheritance all those years ago, and I intend to claim it, although I have no longer any pressing need for it."

"Most dishonorable of him, to be sure," Papa said, sitting back in his chair. "How did that come about, if I may ask?"

"It is not a pretty story, sir; rather, it is one of deceit and betrayal."

"And you said your brother's name was John?" Papa asked when Timothy Ferguson paused and stared thoughtfully at the glowing coals in the grate. "Was he older than you?"

"He was a year younger, but we were enough alike in looks to be taken for twins. That was a long time ago, though; we may have aged differently. However, I'd know him even if fifty years had passed."

My father smiled then, for the first time since the arrival of the other Mr. Ferguson. "Your desire to settle old scores is a strong one, then," he commented.

"Exactly," replied Timothy Ferguson. "You see—well—I guess the trouble was that each of us was bent on outshining the other. We were rivals, you might say. Nothing wrong with that when all is fair and square, but John was not above using devious methods to get what he wanted. I learned that early in life. Oh, he was clever about it—people thought the world of him. We were brought up by an aunt and uncle, a somewhat elderly couple, and as far as they were concerned Johnny could do no wrong. But he was careful that they never saw the side of him that I saw.

"To come to the point: John wanted me out of the way. He was always suggesting that I go out into the world to seek my fortune, saying that I was wasting my time in school, that I should be more adventurous, and so on. He never mentioned Uncle Andrew's money—which I, as the older brother, stood to inherit—but I knew that he could hardly wait to get his hands on it. In the end he succeeded in getting what he wanted."

He paused, as if he needed a moment or two in which to cast his mind back over the years.

"The two of us went off one weekend with a couple of

friends for a few days fishing at a lonely little cove up the Irish coast. We'd gone there any number of times and never met with any trouble, but on that particular occasion we interrupted a band of smugglers who were using the cove to unload their booty from a boat anchored a little way off the shore. They were a rough bunch, and let it be known that they were anything but pleased to see us.

"They dragged the two Muldoon boys and myself—somehow John got away from them—down into the water, and forced us to help pass the chests and boxes along, sort of a bucket brigade. I don't know whether or not they would have let us go after the job was done, but it never came to that. Maybe nothing would have happened to us if someone, and I know it was my brother, hadn't alerted the coastal watch and the constabulary.

"The end result was that the Muldoons and I, along with the smugglers, were tried, found guilty, and deported to Australia."

"How did you know it was your brother who informed on you?" Papa asked.

"First of all, he never came to our defense, when he could easily have explained how we were forced into helping the smugglers. And second, there was his smile, his ugly, satisfied smile when he saw me taken off in chains. He had won, you see."

No one spoke for a few moments, and then our visitor continued.

"A sorry tale, sir, with which to burden you, but I wanted to make clear the reason for my search."

"Of course, yes, of course," Papa said quickly. "I take it you did not fare too badly in Australia in spite of going there as a prisoner. You have the look of a successful man."

"Yes, indeed. There was, and still is, money to be made there, with hard work and a bit of luck. But you may well be wondering how I, a condemned criminal, managed to become wealthy. It happened this way: When the group of us, the smugglers, the Muldoons, and I, were brought before the Australian authorities to be assigned work, the entire case was reviewed. Under questioning, one of the smugglers let it slip that the three of us had been forced into participating in unloading the booty, with the result that we were declared innocent and were free to return to Ireland.

"I do not know what happened to the Muldoons, but I was in no mood to go back to the country that had so unjustly condemned me. Also, I was so angry at my brother that I was afraid I might do him an injury.

"The rest is quickly told. I worked for a sheep rancher for a while, and later on became a rancher myself, a successful one, making more money than I'd ever dreamed possible. I might still be in Australia—I'd come to like it there—but as a sideline I'd bought into an import-export company, and after my wife's death I decided to give up ranching and devote myself to it. New York is definitely the center for that business, so I've come here with my son. That is my prime reason for being here. You might say that my search for my brother, who may very well be dead by now, is incidental. But I would like to find him. To settle the score, you see."

At that moment I glanced at my father and was surprised at the intense concentration with which he stared at our guest. Timothy Ferguson must have taken Papa's expression for one of irritation or disapproval, for he stood up suddenly and apologized again for interrupting our Sunday afternoon.

"If you should happen to hear of any other John Fergusons in this city, sir, I would appreciate your informing me. I am lodged nearby, at the American Hotel, only two doors away from you, for the present. As I said, my son, Ian, is with me, and will take a message if I am not available."

With that he bowed courteously and took his leave. When I returned to the parlor after seeing him out Papa was standing in front of the fireplace, staring fixedly at the Ship's Clock on the mantel, and I knew it was not the time for any discussion or speculation concerning our caller's story.

The "other Ferguson," as I came to think of him, had aroused my curiosity. By his own admission he had no need of the inheritance at this point in his life (perhaps, as he said, it was merely a matter of "settling the score") and his appearance indicated that he could afford the best that money could buy in the matter of dress. I knew that the moment I felt the softness of the light, warm coat he handed to me. An intricately designed gold watch chain that he wore looped across his velvet waistcoat was only partly visible, but I was sure it was a fine, valuable piece. Nor had I failed to note his snow white cravat and starched shirt, both obviously of the finest linen. All this bespoke a man of means, as well as one who knew how to dress richly and still avoid ostentation—a knowledge I intended to acquire.

In the days that followed his visit I kept an eye out for him whenever I passed the American Hotel, but did not see him until a week later. He came into the bank with his son, a tall, good-looking youth whose age I guessed to be nineteen or twenty. The two of them were closeted with Mr. Dillingham, the bank's president, for the better part of an hour, and when at last I saw the door of the corner office open, I closed the window of my teller's cage and pretended to have an errand in the public area of the bank.

Mr. Ferguson greeted me pleasantly, introduced me to his son, and asked if I could direct them to Columbia College, where Ian would like to continue his studies.

"I understand the term is well under way," Ian said with a smile very much like that of his father. "Do you happen to know whether they accept latecomers?"

"No, I am afraid I don't know," I answered, "but my brother James is there, and if you care to look him up I can promise you that he'll be of help."

"Thank you, Robert Ferguson," the father said. "We'll do

51

that. And perhaps you will do me the honor of taking a midday meal with me in the near future."

At supper that night Jay reported that he had met Ian Ferguson and had more or less taken him under his wing.

"And just what does that mean?" Papa asked, frowning down at the cold meat to which he was helping himself.

"Oh, I just showed him around, where to register, and which rooms to go to. He wants to be a lawyer. And we ate together at noon. Nice fellow, Ian is."

"Was his father there?" Papa was still frowning.

"Just at first. When he saw that Ian was admitted, he left."

"Turned him over to you, eh?" Papa's tone was disparaging. "Well, see that you don't find yourself playing nursemaid to the boy—Annetta! Cannot we have a single meal without spilled food? Of all the clumsy—"

"She's still a child, John," Mama intervened. "She didn't mean to do it. Ellen, find a cloth to mop that up. Annetta, stop crying and eat your food. James, pass the potato cakes to your father."

The meal was finished in relative silence, and we were all relieved when Mama stood up, after carefully rolling her napkin into one of the wooden rings Papa had fashioned years ago. He followed her out of the dining room to the parlor, and after a moment the rest of us headed upstairs, knowing it would be advisable to stay out of sight until Papa's mood improved.

It was unlike him to lash out at his favorite, Annetta (we used to say she got away with things we wouldn't dream of doing), and I suspected the reference to the "other Fergusons" had upset him more than the spilled milk. I suggested to Jay that he keep quiet about Ian, and when the senior Ferguson stopped in to chat with me on his next visit to the bank I made no mention of it at home.

Nor did I mention the lunch I had with him at the Bank

Coffee House at 11 Pine Street, where we were served an excellent green turtle soup, oysters on the half shell, broiled hip steak, fried potatoes, and a half bottle of Madeira. I was interested to see that while the soup and oysters were listed at twenty-five cents each, the steak was only twelve and a half cents, and equally good.

In the course of the meal I questioned my host about his life in Australia, hoping to find out how he had made his fortune.

"Yes," he said as we sat over our wine, "I went there many years ago, and not by choice, either, as I told you. But that's beside the point; when I arrived there I was slated to do convict labor, and the future looked pretty dismal. I was fortunate, though, in that the owner of a large sheep ranch was looking for cheap labor, and picked me along with a few other fellows. He liked me, and when he heard my story he gave me every opportunity to better my situation. A good man, he. I worked hard, and after a while struck out on my own. Land was incredibly cheap at the time, and bit by bit I bought up stretches until I had a spread of a thousand acres, give or take a few hundred, and eventually prospered beyond anything I could have hoped for in my native Ireland."

"You acquired the land for farming, sir?" I asked.

"Sheep farming," he said with a nod. "And it turned out to be a most lucrative venture. England, like most of Europe, lacks the room to raise sheep on a large scale, and is only too willing to import all the raw wool she can. The English manufacture cloth in their mills—Australia does little of that—and sell the finished product, both domestically and abroad."

When I inquired whether he still retained his Australian interests, he shook his head.

"No longer. After my wife died last year I sold out." He paused for a moment, and examined his wineglass. "No, I shall not go back there. I propose to set up my import-export business here in the near future, and I want Ian to establish himself in the New World. Tell me, Robert—you are more familiar with New York than I am—is Great Jones Street a desirable address? I'm thinking of taking a house there."

By June of 1833 "the other Fergusons" had left the American Hotel and taken up residence not in Great Jones Street but in Stuyvesant Square over on Second Avenue between Fifteenth and Seventeenth streets, an excellent address. It was just as well they moved when they did, for Andrew Jackson, who had had his second inauguration in March of that year, arrived in New York on June twelfth, and took over the American Hotel for his headquarters. Elaborate preparations had been made for his visit; indeed, the whole neighborhood seemed to be caught up in a frenzy of activity, which came to a head when the president disembarked from the steamboat *North America* at the wharf at Castle Garden. The streets, the stoops, even the housetops were filled with the excited, jubilant people who had turned out to see him. The roar of welcome that went up when he came into view was like nothing I had ever heard before, and must, I thought, have pleased him mightily.

Papa, Jay, and I had come out together (Mama and the girls were made to stay at home for fear they'd be trampled on in the crowds), but in the press of people we had become separated. Later, hot, tired, and hungry, I turned to find Ian Ferguson next to me, wiping his brow. On impulse I asked him to come home with me and refresh himself with a cooling drink, an invitation he accepted readily.

Strange, that a chance meeting like that should have such lasting consequences . . .

Ellen	It was exactly one year ago today, June 12, 1833, that Robert brought Ian Ferguson home with him. I had just turned away from the bow window, from which I'd been watching the throngs of people on Broadway, hoping for a glimpse of President Jackson, when I heard the front door open.
	"Ellen, may I present Mr. Ian Ferguson?" Robert was always proper about introductions. "Ian, this is my sister Ellen. Do be seated. If you will excuse me for a moment I'll see about some refreshments."

Ian smiled—he had a wonderful smile—and said I'd been wise not to venture out in the heat and the crowds.

"Did you see the president?" I asked.

"Yes, for an instant," he replied, "but then he was swallowed up amongst the people surrounding him. There wasn't the slightest chance of meeting him. But I am delighted to make *your* acquaintance, Miss Ellen; your brother Jay pointed you out to me one afternoon when you were crossing the park with another young lady. Do you often walk in the park?"

I had no chance to reply, for at that moment Mama came in with Annetta and little Paul, followed almost immediately by Papa and Jay, making further introductions necessary. Jay greeted Ian warmly—I gathered they saw a good deal of each other at Columbia—but Papa, while he acknowledged our guest politely enough, seemed cool, a bit withdrawn. I noticed, too, that his answers to Mama's questions about the president's arrival were short, almost to the point of curtness. Nor did he join in the general conversation.

I saw Ian glance at me from time to time as we sat drinking the iced apple cider Anna brought in, but I had no further conversation with him that afternoon, and after a suitable interval he made ready to leave. Jay saw him to the door, and when he returned to the parlor I thought he looked at me quizzically for a moment before sitting down again.

"What a well-mannered young man that is!" Mama exclaimed, taking Paul up on her lap. "Did you see how politely he thanked me for our hospitality, John?"

Papa did not answer her; instead, he stood up abruptly and looked at my older brothers.

"James and Robert, come with me," he said gruffly, and led the two startled young men out of the parlor and up the stairs.

"Papa gave no reason, none at all, Ellen," Jay said to me when we were both up on the third floor after dinner. "He merely said that we were to have no further communication with either Ian or his father. I can't imagine why. Robert says Mr. Ferguson is a splendid man, and I can see nothing wrong with Ian. When I said that I couldn't very well pretend not to know him at school, Papa said I would have to do just that, and then he stalked out of the room. Of course I will see Ian just as usual."

"I can't understand it, Jay," I said. "Mama liked him, and I . . ."

"And Ian was taken with you, sister dear. When I went to the door with him he asked me if I thought he might call on you. Naturally I said yes, but now—"

"Jay, will you walk with me in the park tomorrow afternoon?" I asked.

Because of the president's visit the park was unusually crowded the next afternoon, and I had almost given up hope of seeing Ian when Jay nudged me.

"Why, what do you know!" he exclaimed in mock surprise. "There's Ian Ferguson, and he seems to be headed this way."

Ian didn't bother to pretend that this was an unexpected meeting. "I was hoping to run into someone I knew," he said happily, bowing to me after clapping Jay on the shoulder. I was slightly embarrassed, though, when, after a few minutes of light conversation, Jay suddenly remembered an important errand and hurried away. Ian, however, looked pleased and offered me his arm, asking if I would join him for tea.

"I've heard that Niblo's Garden has a reputation for good food," he said, "but I've not been there myself. Do you know it at all?"

"Oh, yes," I answered as we started to make our way out of the park. "Niblo's is famous, and quite respectable." I'd never been there myself, but Margit van Eyck had spoken highly of it. Her father occasionally took her family to Sunday dinner there.

I felt quite elegant, sitting across from Ian at one of the little tables that were shaded by vine-covered trellises, pouring the tea he ordered and feeling his eyes on me.

"We were in the habit of having tea every afternoon in Australia," he said, helping himself to milk and sugar. "Do you have the same custom?"

"We sometimes have it at home," I replied, "but my parents generally prefer coffee."

"Oh, would you rather have that? I could order—"

"No, indeed. I like coffee at breakfast, and after dinner, but not otherwise."

I cannot recall everything we talked about that day, but I remember that we talked a good deal, that there were no awkward silences either during our little repast or on the walk back up to 233 Broadway. And of course I remember that Ian asked if he might call on me later in the week.

"I study in the evenings," he said, frowning slightly, "so—"

"Oh, the afternoon is preferable," I said quickly, mindful of my father's injunction. "My parents do not like us to go out at night. They consider the streets unsafe then."

"The afternoon it shall be," he said, smiling down at me. "Would Tuesday suit you?"

Tuesday suited me very well, as did several other afternoons early that summer.

In the middle of July a second epidemic of cholera caused a general exodus from the city and put an end to my clandestine meetings with Ian. He and his father went to a hunting lodge in the mountains, and we went back to the house in Rockaway. I was unable to communicate with him during the seven long weeks we were away, and as time went on I became more and more fearful that our brief, innocent romance was over, sure that he'd forget all about me.

When he appeared on our doorstep the day after we returned to New York, however, one look at his face assured me that I had worried needlessly. As usual, Papa was at work, and Mama happened to be busy upstairs when he came, so I was able to slip out unobserved. That was the day I told Ian what Papa had said to Robert and Jay the day of President Jackson's arrival. He looked perplexed for a moment, and then he smiled and tucked my arm in his.

"But he didn't forbid *you* to see me, did he, Ellen?" he asked with a little laugh. "And if he does, I shall find a way—oh, darling, I know it's too soon to say this to you—but do you know the poet's line 'Whoever loved that loved not at first sight'?"

With that he pressed my arm close to his side and said we were going to his house on Stuyvesant Square. He wanted me to meet his father.

By the end of September we were as deeply in love as it is possible for two people to be, and so intent on being together that we paid little attention to the rest of the world. In spite of having to dissemble, to pretend I was spending my time with Margit or Bettina, and even in spite of having to lie, I was happier than I'd ever dreamed of being, and wouldn't have had a care in the world if it hadn't been for Papa.

I was terrified that he would find me out and lock me in my room, or take some equally drastic measure. Only when I was in bed at night would I let myself think of Ian, of the eager look in his eyes when he saw me approaching, of the pressure of his hand on my arm when he helped me in or out of a carriage, or the warmth of his embrace on the few occasions when we were alone. I was afraid I'd look as moonstruck as Robert did whenever Bettina's name was mentioned.

Ian was too self-confident to let Papa's refusal to receive him upset him the way it did me. "As long as I'm sure of you, my dearest," he said one rainy October afternoon when we were having tea in one of the parlors of the Holt Hotel in Fulton Street (a safe distance from home). "I don't care what anyone else thinks. Your father will either come around in the end, or he won't. And if he does not, it will be his loss. With any luck we'll be able to marry in a couple of years, maybe sooner. I finish at the college in June, and then I shall read law in some firm. But tell me this, Ellen: Would you be willing to be cut off from your family if marrying me meant that?"

"Yes, of course," I answered, "although I'd rather not be. And maybe it won't work out that way; we'd always be able to see Robert and Jay, and perhaps I can see Mama and the young ones when Papa's at the shop. At least *your* father seemed to have no objection to me when you took me to meet him."

"No, indeed. He liked you very much, dearest. He just shrugged when I told him what your Pa had said to Robert and Jay, and said not to let it worry me."

"Well, I'm glad we don't have to hide from him, Ian. You've no idea what a conniving, deceitful person I've become. Right now I'm supposed to be spending the afternoon with Margit, and look at me—"

"All in a good cause, my dearest."

"Heavens! Look at the time! It's after five—will you walk me part of the way home? No, don't call a carriage. If they see it driving up they'll ask questions—and we can both fit under my umbrella."

In spite of the lateness of the hour we took our time walking home, and just before we turned the corner into Broadway, Ian drew me into a doorway where he held the umbrella up as a shield against the eyes of passersby while he kissed me. Later I straightened my bonnet, and after promising to meet him again in two days' time went the rest of the way alone, unable to think of anything other than the pressure of his lips on mine. I must have looked like a somnambulist.

"Ellen, is that you?" Mama called from the dining room as soon as I entered the house. "Come to supper, Liebchen; Papa sent word he would be late tonight, so we are having an early meal. I hope you did not fill yourself up on cakes and tarts at Margit's."

"No, Mama, we just had tea," I answered, glancing at Jay, who pretended to be engrossed in unfolding his napkin. Dear Jay, he knew very well where I'd been.

It was just as well that Papa wasn't at the table that night: Paul knocked his soup bowl from the tray of his child's chair, and Annetta upset the gravy boat when Robert asked her to pass it to him. Mama sighed and asked me to find a cloth, but she didn't scold. Later, when we were eating Anna's apple strudel still warm from the oven, Jay made us all laugh with a wicked imitation of a professor who talked out of one side of his mouth. But that was the last time there was any laughter in our house for weeks—or maybe it was months.

I was in the parlor helping Annetta with her spelling words when it happened. Robert was sitting under one of the gas fixtures reading the paper, and Mama had taken Paul upstairs. I don't know where Jay was. All evening I had been conscious of street noises, shouts, whistles, and the sound of running feet, but I paid little attention to them, since demonstrations in connection with the coming mayoral election had been going on for days. The supporters of Gulian Verplanck, the Whig candidate, did not campaign as vigorously as the Democrats did for Cornelius Lawrence, one of Bettina's uncles. The Tammany Hall Irish, on the other hand, were said to spend their evenings rounding up votes amongst the lower classes, using threats and money to get them to vote not once, but many times. I wonder how Mr. Lawrence felt about that. Bettina never mentioned politics.

Annetta was yawning over the last of the words on her list when we heard heavy footsteps close to the house, followed by a sharp, loud knocking on the front door. By the time I reached the hallway Robert had the door wide open and was trying to help two members of the city militia carry my father into the house. I had only a quick look at him before he was borne upstairs, but it was time enough for me to see that blood was streaming down over his face, and that his hair was covered with mud or blood; in that light it was hard to tell which. His arms were hanging limply, like those on Annetta's rag doll, I thought somewhat hysterically.

Someone must have sent for Dr. Bogert, and after he arrived the two soldiers came downstairs and told us what had happened. Papa had been waylaid, they said, by a gang of ruffians known as the Dead Rabbits, a particularly rough band of men, and beaten senseless with clubs and brickbats.

"A wild bunch they are," the taller of the two men said. "Mr. Ferguson probably refused to give them his purse when they grabbed him—that's what they do, you see. They accost respectable-looking people and demand their money. And if you don't pay them they trample on you and rub your face in the mud; sometimes they break your bones. They should all be in jail."

"How badly hurt is he?" Robert asked.

The soldier couldn't say, but some time later Dr. Bogert came down and said he would send in a nurse.

"Is he awake?" Jay wanted to know.

"Yes, he has regained consciousness," the doctor replied, "and the cuts and bruises, while painful, do not appear to be serious. It's his leg I'm worried about; it looks to me as if the kneecap has been badly injured. I'll be back in the morning with a colleague of mine for another look. In the meantime the nurse will take over.

"Now: Ellen, go up to your mother, and keep the little ones out of the way. You two boys go and sit with your father until the nurse comes. Keep him from moving that leg. He's uncomfortable, and will probably complain, but don't panic. He's not going to die."

As Dr. Bogert had foretold, the cuts and bruises healed quickly, leaving Papa with only a slight scar on his forehead, but in spite of all the doctors could do, his leg continued to trouble him for the rest of his life. Never a man known for his patience, Papa insisted on returning to the shop less than two weeks after the beating, contrary, of course, to the doctor's instructions to keep off his right foot for another month.

"Where will the business go without me?" he expostulated to Mama when she urged him to stay home. "Who, I ask you, will provide for you? Enough, Maria. I know my own strength better than any doctor does, and I will do things my way.

"James, I want you to purchase a cane for me, a good stout one, either ebony or ash. Ellen, I will expect you to come to the shop with me, and help with the paperwork; you have been idle long enough. Robert, you will walk with us in the morning and appear at Maiden Lane when you finish at the bank in the evening to accompany us home. That will be the arrangement until the first of the year, when James will escort us. Yes, James! You will finish out this term at college, and in January you will begin working for me and preparing—"

"But, Papa—" Jay protested.

"Do not interrupt me! You will be preparing to take over the business. Do you think I am going to go on slaving for you forever? Besides, you've had enough schooling, any more is unnecessary. Ellen and Robert, be ready to leave with me at half past eight tomorrow morning."

| James | I do not look back on 1835 as a year filled with fond memories, and neither, I am sure, does Ellen. We trudged off with Papa, day after monotonous day, to the house in which we had spent so many years, a house renovated now into a place of business, and bearing little resemblance to the home it once was. The large black range was still in the old kitchen, and on the wall next to it the marks we had made years ago when measuring our heights were still visible behind the worktables of the apprentices, but I could find no |

other sign that we had ever lived there.

From the first I felt as if I had taken a step in the wrong direction, and it was not a pleasant feeling. The once cheerful rooms were not only dreary and dusty (Ellen said the house inhaled dust and dirt from the street), but also loud with the noise and vibrations of the presses and cutting machines. An enterprise that should have occupied a large, open space in a commercial building or factory was crowded into three floors of small, inconvenient rooms, where workers were continually getting in one another's way.

Since the first pair of suspenders had been sold to a fireman the business had grown rapidly and steadily, primarily because Papa had kept adding items to his inventory, some turned out in quantity, and some made to order. He hadn't liked the cane I bought for him—said it was poor workmanship—and immediately set about designing a whole line of walking sticks for both men and women. Some were plain polished wood with curved handles that fitted neatly into the hand. Others were carved and decorated with emblems; I remember an old lady ordering one with a likeness of her pet parrot placed where she could stroke it with her forefinger as she walked along.

For himself Papa produced by far the ugliest cane I ever saw, a knobby, heavy walking stick, over an inch in diameter, approximately four feet long, and fitted with a plain brass handle—but more of that later.

My duties were never clearly defined; I simply filled in wherever an extra hand was needed, ran errands, waited on customers who came into the shop (the old parlor), took turns at various machines, and tried to keep out of Papa's way. What I hated most was being sent down to the cellar to operate one of the machines for a long, long day when a workman failed to show up. The endless repetition nearly drove me out of my mind.

Ellen was not much better off. Papa set her to work in the little room, the old "home office" behind the parlor, where she struggled with the correspondence and the haphazard system of bookkeeping he had set up. Fortunately she had a head for figures, but it was clear to me that she was bored, disinterested, and, as time went on, increasingly resentful. I wondered how long she'd put up with the situation; I knew *I* did not intend to stand it much longer, that I was simply biding my time until I could see a way out. Perhaps Ellen was doing the same thing. She was head over heels in love with Ian, and since

I could no longer carry messages between them, they had difficulty arranging to meet, as well as little time to spend together. I was not in love at the time, and I'm just as glad; it would only have complicated things.

Nothing much ever relieved the monotony of the work, but one hot afternoon in August when Ellen and I were arranging a display of decorative medalions that could be fitted to the doors of carriages, a compact-looking gentleman, dressed all in black and carrying a satchel, came in and asked for Herr Ferguson. I fetched Papa and followed him back into the shop, only to stop abruptly on the threshold when the stranger exclaimed "Philip! Philip!," and threw his arms around my father. Papa was visibly startled, but he said nothing; he merely took the man by the arm and hurried him into the little office.

"Did he call Papa 'Philip'?" Ellen asked, wrinkling her brow. "Did I hear him correctly?"

"Yes, you did," I replied. "He was probably confused. Did you notice his accent? He's a stranger in town."

"But Papa seemed to know him—"

"Maybe he did business with him at some time. Here, put the rest of these in a drawer; there's no more room in the showcase."

At closing time that day Papa introduced us to the foreigner as his cousin Hans, the son of his mother's brother, and said he would be staying with us for a few days.

"We were in school together," Papa said, "good friends always, and now he has come here on business, and of course to renew his acquaintance with me. He also knows your mother. His English is not very good, but if you speak slowly he may understand you. You are to make him welcome, understand?"

I thought the cousin looked uncomfortable, but then Papa was not known for setting people at their ease. Mama was much better at it, and brought smiles to Cousin Hans's face as she chattered away in German to him all through dinner that night. Papa took only a small part in their conversation, and afterward, when we were all amused at the delight our guest took in watching "das Schiff," as he called the clock on the mantelpiece, Papa warned him sharply not to touch it.

"What *is* the matter with Papa?" Ellen asked. "How can he be such a wretched host? Cousin Hans looked so hurt."

"Perhaps he doesn't like him," Robert offered. "Just because he's a cousin doesn't mean—"

"But common politeness, Robert."

"Oh, I agree it's inexcusable, but something must be wrong. Papa never speaks German, and I heard him and Mama talking away to Cousin Hans as soon as I left the parlor—I mean when I was on the stairs," Robert went on. "I couldn't understand what they were saying, of course, but it surely sounded as if they were disagreeing about something. Before that, though, Mama asked me where the Wilkins Brothers had their office, and then she repeated the directions to Cousin Hans in German. He must have some connection with shipping, because the Wilkins are agents for a couple of European lines. They keep a substantial balance at City National."

"Maybe Papa did business with Cousin Hans before Ferguson and Lamb failed," I said, watching Ellen open the drawer to her desk. Her room was the largest and most comfortable of the third-floor bedrooms, and the three of us often gathered there in the evening as soon as we could conveniently leave the parlor.

"His last name is Mesner," Robert said idly, stretching his long legs out in front of him. "I saw it on the tag on his satchel."

"I don't believe he's a cousin at all," Ellen said. "What was Papa's mother's name before she married a Ferguson? I don't think I ever heard it."

We shook our heads, and then suddenly Robert began to

laugh. "Do you realize, little sister, that if you marry Ian your name will be Ellen Ferguson-Ferguson?" he asked softly.

"I always thought hyphenated names were elegant," she retorted. "Now, go to bed, both of you. I have a letter to write."

Cousin Hans was such an unobtrusive guest that when he left us at the end of a fortnight we hardly noticed his absence. We never saw him during the day except at breakfast and dinner, and in the evening he either retired early, or else sat talking quietly to Mama in German. The day he sailed I went with him and Papa down to the dock, only because I was needed to carry the satchel and some of the boxes of presents he had bought for his family. Our farewells at the gangplank were formal, almost perfunctory, a handshake and an *Auf Wiedersehen,* and then he walked quickly away—looking, I thought, like a disappointed man. I never heard Papa speak of him again.

As the rest of the summer dragged by at the pace of a glacier making its way across a barren plain, my restlessness and discontent increased by the day. By the time the first cool days of autumn were upon us I knew that if I wanted to keep control of my temper and my sanity I would have to find a way to break the hold Papa had on me. But what to do? I had saved every penny from the small salary he paid me, but still had far too little to start on a business venture of my own, or to complete my studies at Columbia, which I had begun with the idea of becoming a doctor.

Ian Ferguson was better off than I: He had concentrated on the law while at school, and was by that time reading law in the offices of Willebrandt and Pyne, with the expectation of being taken into the firm as soon as he passed the examination for the bar. He was also blessed with an understanding parent.

I considered various ways of supporting myself, and made a short list of possibilities:

1. Run away to a distant city, Washington or Boston, and find work in a hospital.
2. Join a traveling theater group or a circus.
3. Sign on as a deckhand on a freighter.
4. Become a member of the city militia.

The first option was the only one that appealed to me, and I was thinking about it seriously when things came to a head in an unexpected way.

December 16, 1835, was a bad day from the start. When Ellen and I were walking down to the shop, with Papa limping along between us, I incurred his wrath by slipping on a wet cobblestone and splashing muddy water on his trousers as I fell into a puddle. Before I could pick myself up I heard Ellen scream, and turning my head, I saw that Papa had raised his heavy walking stick, as if he intended to bring it down on my back.

"Get up, you clumsy fool!" he muttered between clenched teeth. "Go back to the house and fetch me another pair of trousers! And clean yourself up. Get on with you!"

By the time I reached the shop the hatred I felt for him had reached the boiling point, and I vowed that that would be the last day I would ever spend under his thumb. And, as things turned out, it was.

About nine o'clock that night a fire that had started in a dry goods store in Merchant Street spread swiftly throughout the lower part of Manhattan, the most destructive conflagration the city had ever known. Naturally everyone ran out to watch; I remember that Robert and I stood with Mr. Hone in Hanover Square for a while before going our separate ways. The flames leapt from building to building with such speed that all the fire-fighting equipment the city could muster was rendered useless. Wall Street was a shambles; all that was left of the impressive Merchants' Exchange were its marble columns, and every building between it and Coenties Slip went up in flames the like of which I hope I never see again.

I don't know what possessed me—probably residual anger over the events of the morning—but suddenly I raced up to Maiden Lane, half hoping to see the shop on fire. The flames had not reached that street, and the shop was intact, but I could see that looters, under cover of the smoke that hung over everything, had smashed the door of number 19 and were carrying off an assortment of goods. I did nothing to stop them; I simply stood and watched, unbelieving and at the same time fascinated by what I saw. I couldn't have been standing there in that trancelike state more than a few minutes when suddenly I was struck such a heavy blow across the shoulders that I fell to the ground for the second time that day.

"Idiot! Oaf!" my father shouted. "Why are you doing nothing to stop the robbers? Get up! Go for the police!"

He stood over me for a moment, and then hobbled into the shop as fast as his bad leg would permit. I saw him shift his grasp on that cruel cane of his so that when he swung it the brass handle would punish his victim severely. Before I turned away I heard a scream, and knew without having seen it what had happened.

I ignored his order to find help and made my way slowly through the disorderly crowds. Mama was still up, waiting for news of the fire, and after describing what I had seen (omitting any reference to Maiden Lane) I said I was going to bed. I was halfway up the stairs when I heard the Ship's Clock strike midnight. I knew then what I would do, and smiled to myself as I went on up to the third floor.

Had it been anyone other than Ellen who knocked on my door a little while later I would have pretended to be asleep. As it was, I sat down with her, and we talked for almost an hour.

70

Ellen	When it was discovered that Jay had not only disappeared on the night of the Great Fire but also taken the Ship's Clock with him, Papa was too concerned about restoring the shop to rights than to do more than denounce him as a thief, and to forbid his name ever to be mentioned in the household. To his surprise, my ordinarily soft-spoken mother flared up angrily when he made that pronouncement.

"I will say his name any time I wish to say it, John Ferguson! You and you alone are responsible for this! Your treatment of him is the cause of his leaving! And you don't care! You mourn the loss of your precious clock more than the loss of your son. And remember, John, this is not the first time it was stolen—"

"Enough, Maria—"

"No, it is not enough! I am ashamed of you. Can you not see that you are following in the footsteps of your own father? But you cannot stop me; I shall speak of James as much as I like."

Papa turned white. I had never before seen him look frightened, but that's how he appeared just then. He said nothing further, and a few minutes later he threw down his napkin and rose from the table.

"Come, Ellen," he said crossly, "and you, Robert. You will walk with us today."

It may have been Jay's defection, or perhaps it was Mama's spirited outbreak, that gave me the courage to say I preferred to stay at home. Papa looked surprised for a moment, and then agreed that it would be better for me to wait until the shop had been restored to order before I returned.

A short time later I went upstairs and took the little pearl ring Ian had given me from its box and slipped it on my finger. I admired it for a moment, and then packed a small case with a few essential articles of clothing. I found my cloak and bonnet, and after a last look around the pleasant bedroom I went downstairs to find my mother. She was startled when she saw my case, but when I showed her the ring she smiled and hugged me.

"This will be a sad household without you and James, Ellen dear," she said with a rueful shake of her head. "It is not easy for me to lose two of my children at once—or even one at a time—but it was bound to happen. And what kind of mother would I be if I tried to keep you here with me when your happiness, and also Jay's, lies elsewhere?"

She straightened my bonnet, and then kissed me lightly on the forehead.

"Be happy, Liebchen," she said with a little smile. "You go with my blessing. Ian is a fine young man."

A strange feeling came over me when I realized I was leaving number 233 for good, and I went slowly down the front steps. She was watching me from the bow window, and when I saw the tears streaming down her cheeks I started to go back into the house, but she forced a smile and motioned to me to go on. I did so, unhurriedly, close to tears myself.

	After Jay disappeared and Ellen eloped with Ian Ferguson, I was of no mind to continue living at 233 Broadway. My mother made a valiant effort to dispel the gloom that enveloped the house like a dense fog when my father was present, and although I did my best to help her by relating anything even remotely humorous or interesting that had happened at the bank that day, the atmosphere in the dining room and later on in the parlor remained decidedly strained.

Robert

Annetta and Paul, young as they were, had sense enough to be on their best behavior and to keep out of the way as much as possible. I remember envying them when I saw them scamper upstairs to their own rooms as soon as they were released from the dinner table, and wishing I could walk out the front door for good.

Unfortunately, though, I was still not in a position to marry Bettina Lawrence and set up a household of my own. I felt it essential that I have a solid financial foundation before I took on the responsibilities of a family man, and the investments I had made in three percents, although sound, were not yet large enough to give me an adequate return. It would be, I figured, another two or three years before I could afford the luxury of a wife and home of my own. It seemed like an interminable wait, and I couldn't be sure that Bettina would not become impatient with the delay and throw me over for some more prosperous fellow. If that happened, I thought, I would probably become as morose and disagreeable as my father, and then no one would have me, ever . . .

Ironically, the fire, which caused an estimated seventeen million dollars in property and business losses, proved in the long run to be of great financial benefit to me. I had escorted Papa to his shop one morning about six weeks after the disaster, and since I had about half an hour before I was due at City National (which fortunately had not been damaged), I wandered over to the streets below Wall Street to see what remained of the area that had suffered the worst of the fire.

Few people were about at that hour, and as I walked along Water Street, viewing the devastation, I was surprised to come upon an elderly couple standing silently in front of a pile of ashes and rubble. The man, dressed in a worn overcoat, had his arm around the woman, whose shoulders seemed to be shaking. At the sound of my approach he turned: I saw that his thin face was lined and his faded blue eyes filled with tears of despair.

When I asked if I could be of any assistance, the woman, who had been too wrapped up in her grief to be aware of my presence, turned slowly, shaking her head.

"If you can restore our house to us, young man—" she began.

"Now, Lisbet," her husband interrupted, "no need to be sharp; he means well. You see that pile of rubble, sir? That was our home, and the pile next door? That one we owned, too, and with the rent it brought we could live. But with both of them gone—"

"And no one to turn to," the woman said bitterly. "We've been over a month in the almshouse, young man, but we can stand that no longer. Conditions there are not for the likes of us, what with the vermin and the filth and the poor food. It's a wonder we're still walking around."

"No, we shan't go back there," the old man said. "We'd either starve or die of disease. It's a terrible place. The dead are sometimes left for two or three days before being taken away. And the morals! Even though they are diseased, prostitutes ply their trade on bundles of straw. There is no order: The alcoholics, the blind, and the crippled are all thrown together! And the stench! It destroys any appetite for the loathsome food they hand out."

"Have you not eaten this morning?" I asked. "No? Come, then, with me. There's a coffee shop not far . . ."

"You are kind, sir, but we cannot pay, nor can we—"

"Oh, Jan," the wife wailed, "you need, we *need* food; do you want to drop dead in the street from weakness?"

"Come," I said, taking each one by the arm and starting back the way I had come. "I am hungry, too. We'll see what Herr Frankel has to offer at his shop this morning."

I will be the first to admit that any kindness I showed Mr. and Mrs. Underbach was not entirely from altruistic motives, although I did genuinely pity the poor old couple. I had been on the lookout for money-making prospects all my life, and my instincts told me that their rubble-filled property, so close to the financial center of the city, was bound to appreciate in value as time went on. I saw there a God-given opportunity to become a landowner at a price I could afford, an opportunity I could not resist.

Over a hearty breakfast of ham, eggs, sausage, porridge, and bread in a corner of the coffee shop on Hanover Street the

Underbachs became a bit more cheerful, but not unnaturally the conversation kept returning to the hopelessness of their situation. I learned that they'd had two sons, both of whom were dead, one of the cholera, and the other lost at sea, leaving them with no living relatives except a brother of Mrs. Underbach in Holland.

"Otto is a kind, good man," she said, "and he would take us in, I know, but how do we get to Amsterdam? We have no money."

"And no way of raising any," added her husband.

"Would you consider selling the land your two houses occupied?" I asked cautiously.

"Ach, and who would buy?" Mr. Underback dismissed my suggestion with a wave of his hand.

"Hm-m," I said, shaking my head, as if realizing that finding a buyer would be no easy task. "It would take money to clear the land and build."

"And who can afford that now?" he argued. "The fire has wiped out everyone—"

"If we could sell it, Jan," his wife broke in, "for whatever we could get, enough for the passage to Holland, where we could live in peace with Otto and his daughters—"

"If, if, if!" the old man was almost shouting. "And what do we do while we wait for a buyer? Tell me that, and stop dreaming of Holland. I can think of nothing but the almshouse again."

"No, no, Jan!" Mrs. Underbach pleaded, turning her head away from me to hide the tears that threatened.

It seemed the right moment to make my offer.

"I have a solution," I said slowly. "Let us find out the cost of the passage to Amsterdam, and then if you are willing, I will give you the money for it in exchange for your land on Water Street."

Stunned by my suggestion, Mr. Underbach stared at me

speechless while his wife all but embraced me in her excitement.

"You are either a fool or a saint, young sir," the old man said finally, "but before you come to your senses, let us go and see when a ship is due to sail."

I cannot say I am proud of what I did, but I assuaged my conscience for taking such blatant advantage of the Underbachs by putting them up at Mrs. Howe's boarding house on Ann Street until the *DeWitt Clinton* was ready to weigh anchor. I didn't know what else to do with them; I couldn't leave them on the streets, nor, with Papa in his current mood, could I take them home. The cost of their lodging was reasonable enough, and I could easily afford it, but their gratitude was so overwhelming that I kept away from them as much as I could until it was time for them to board the ship.

Although the entire operation had reduced my net worth considerably, I still felt my investment to be a sound one. The cabin (I would have felt worse had I permitted them to go steerage) cost me a hundred and fifty dollars, the bill at the boarding house amounted to only nine dollars (three dollars a day for three days), and the clerk at City Hall charged me five dollars to register the deed to the property in my name.

As I stood on the dock, watching the *DeWitt Clinton* go out on the tide, I saw the old couple looking much as I had first seen them, he with his arm around her—the only difference being that this time they were smiling and waving happily. I turned away, even happier than they were: I was a landowner! I was the rightful holder of valuable real estate, and all it had cost me was one hundred and sixty-four dollars! The warm woolen shawl I gave to Mrs. Underbach I had found in Ellen's chest.

I might easily have forgotten the date of the Underbach's departure for Holland, January 31, 1836, had it not been for what took place in the parlor of 233 Broadway that very night.

It had begun to snow around midday, and I was cold and tired when I reached home later than usual. I had stayed on after closing hour at the bank to make up for the time I had taken to see the Dutch couple safely on board the ship, and dinner was well under way when I took my place at the table. Papa merely nodded when I said I'd been working on a plan my superior wished to present to the board of directors the next day (this was only partly true; I'd also been catching up on my own work). He said that when I finished eating I was to clear the snow from the stoop and the walk in front of the house.

"Could it not wait until tomorrow, John?" Mama asked. "Robert has had a long day. He is tired—"

"So he is tired!" Papa exclaimed. "I am also tired; I, too, have had a long day. But he is young, Maria, and I am not. Do you want *me* to shovel the snow?"

"Papa, I'll *do* it," I said hastily. "Paul, you can take the small broom and sweep up what I miss."

Paul, who was by then a sturdy five-year-old, did his part competently, stopping only occasionally to make a snowball and hurl it across Broadway.

"Not much sense in doing this," he observed when we had nearly finished. "Look how it's coming down! It will be all covered up again by morning, and we'll have it all to do over again."

Before I had time to answer him, a sleigh drawn by two fine-looking horses drew up in front of the house, and a moment later Mr. Timothy Ferguson alighted. He instructed the driver to wait for him, and then bade us a cheerful good evening.

"Well, young Robert, you are looking fit," he said with a smile, "and I see you have a fine fellow as an assistant." He nodded to Paul, and then turned back to me. "Is your father at home? If so, I should like to see him."

"Yes, sir," I answered, glancing at the light that shone out through the bow window, "but—"

"I understand your hesitation, Robert; I also understand that he will not be anxious to receive me. But the time has come to clear up whatever misunderstanding has caused him to take the position he has. Will you be kind enough to show me in?"

I saw no way of refusing his request, and after we watched Paul toss one last snowball out into the darkness, the three of us entered the house together.

Some of the details of the painful scene that followed escape me now, but the overall picture is deeply imprinted on my mind, so deeply that I doubt that I shall ever be able to blot it out, much as I would like to expunge the memory of it.

Mr. Timothy Ferguson wasted no time in stating the purpose of his visit; he waited only long enough to greet Mama before beginning to speak.

"I have come, sir," he said, in the manner of one who has a carefully prepared speech in mind, "in the hope of rectifying any misunderstanding that exists between us. Our families, united now by the marriage of your daughter Ellen to my son Ian—"

"I no longer have a daughter Ellen!" Papa thundered. He had risen from his armchair when we entered the room, and stood leaning on his walking stick, his eyes cold with anger. "And I have forbidden the members of my family to have any communication with her."

"Perhaps, sir, you will reconsider when I tell you—"

"You can tell me nothing that will alter my decision."

"I can understand your displeasure at her marrying without your consent, but the marriage is a happy one, and soon—"

"Enough!" Papa said loudly. "You are wasting your time. You came here uninvited, and I demand that you remove yourself at once. Go!"

When our visitor made no move to leave, Papa, his eyes blazing, started to raise his stick. Mama gasped and caught hold of his arm, causing him to lose his balance and fall heavily to the floor.

It is the memory of my father lying on the carpet in the parlor, defeated by his own wrath, that haunts me at times. No one spoke, and no one dared to go near him. He lay still for at least sixty seconds, then he raised himself partially and pointed toward the door.

"Out! Out!" he roared. "All of you, out, out, out!"

Mama, Paul, and Annetta almost stumbled over one another as they beat a hasty retreat while Mr. Timothy Ferguson and I followed more slowly, appalled by what we had seen.

"My apologies, ma'am," Mr. Ferguson said to Mama once we were out in the hall. "I thought now that some time had elapsed and that Ellen—"

An angry groan from the parlor caused him to break off; he turned to the outer door of the vestibule, and as he did so he pressed a card into my hand, whispering, "Come when you can."

It was almost three weeks before I could comply with his request. The day following his visit the city was at a standstill; the snow continued to fall, piling up drifts against the stoops and railings, and covering the streets to a depth of two or more feet. We could see no sign of life on Broadway from the bow window, nothing but a great white expanse. I remember Mama saying how clean and lovely the snow made the city look, but all I could think of was what a mess it would make once it began to melt.

No mention was made of Papa's fall the night before, but since he kept to his room all day, emerging only at dinnertime looking haggard and drawn, I was quite sure he had suffered a further injury to his bad knee.

"The storm will blow itself out over night," he said toward

the end of the meal, "and I wish you to arise at six tomorrow morning, Robert, to clear the stoop again so that I can get out. Then go to the livery stables on John Street, and arrange for a sleigh to come for me at eight o'clock. If you are not there early they will all be spoken for, so perhaps it would be better if you arose at five o'clock."

He was right about the weather, and also right about the demand for sleighs. I arose in darkness, and dressed in my warmest clothes, I started in on the stoop, barely able to see what I was doing. It took me longer than I had anticipated to make a path down the steps—I made no attempt to clear them completely—and by the time I arrived at the stables all the sleighs save one were taken. The hostler agreed to have it at 233 Broadway by eight o'clock, but when I saw the sorry-looking nag that was to pull it I wondered . . .

I had difficulty making my way back to the house; in spite of my heavy boots and woolen gloves my feet and hands soon lost all sensation in the bitter cold that had set in after the storm. My face felt so stiff that I thought the skin would crack if I moved my jaw, and by the time I reached our front door I was unutterably, unbearably weary. Mama took one look at me as I stumbled into the hallway and ordered me to bed for the rest of the day. I was halfway up the stairs when I heard Papa protest that if he could go to work, I could, too, but for once Mama overruled him. I never did hear whether the sleigh arrived on time.

I do not remember much about the next few days; Mama told me later that Dr. Bogert had come and said I was suffering from exhaustion and fever, and should remain quiet for at least a fortnight. It was not until the last Sunday in February, therefore, that I was able to present myself at Mr. Timothy Ferguson's residence on Stuyvesant Square.

Ellen, looking prettier than ever, greeted me at the door with genuine affection and enthusiasm, and led me into a spacious parlor where her husband and father-in-law awaited us. In the course of the afternoon's conversation I learned that she and Ian were living with T. F. (which is what they both called Ian's father) more or less on a permanent basis, which rather surprised me. I would, I thought, value my independence too much ever to live with Bettina's father.

T. F. may have had some inkling of my thoughts, for after a glance in my direction he explained that his import-export business necessitated frequent trips abroad.

"And but for Ellen and Ian," he continued, smiling at the young couple, "this house, which I need as a home base, would stand empty for almost three quarters of the time. As it is, I need have no concern about it when I am away; Ellen has taken charge and runs the establishment as smoothly as clockwork.

"But let me get on to the matter I wished to discuss with you, Robert. Even before Ellen and Ian were married, your father's attitude to me was anything but friendly. Why is that? I have searched my mind for a legitimate reason, and can find none. Did I offend him in some way of which I am unaware the day I called thinking he might be my brother John?"

"I was not present that day, T. F.," Ellen said, "but I cannot imagine your saying anything offensive. Robert—"

"Yes, I was there," I said, "and I can assure you in all honesty, sir, that you neither did nor said anything that might be interpreted as a slur or insult."

"But," Ellen interposed, "wasn't it after that—yes, it was when you brought Ian home the day of President Jackson's visit to New York—that Papa forbade any communication between the families."

"Then I must be to blame," Ian said. "For some reason he took a dislike to me then and there—I could tell by the way he looked at me—but he couldn't have known then that I would steal you away from him."

"I think," I said slowly, "that it goes back to T. F.'s first visit. Papa did not act like his normal self that day. I remember

82

thinking he looked apprehensive, as if he scented some sort of danger."

"I certainly had no intention of making him uncomfortable," T. F. said apologetically. "Perhaps I should have left as soon as I realized he was not my brother."

"I wonder if it was your story that upset him, sir; about your brother's betrayal of you. Could that have reminded him of something in his past? Ellen, did you ever hear of anything similar?"

"No," she answered, "but then you know how little Papa ever spoke of his past. He didn't like us to ask about it; he'd become cross if we did. He's always been short-tempered, come to think of it, and since the injury to his knee—remember, Ian, that I told you how he'd been beaten up by one of the street gangs? He's been in pain ever since, and that hasn't helped his disposition . . ."

"Exactly," I said when she seemed to hesitate. "And since James took off with the Ship's Clock—"

"And then I eloped—"

"Undoubtedly your father has had a series of shocks," T. F. said, "which may account for his behavior when I called the second time—"

"His behavior was completely inexcusable," I broke in. "I cannot understand it at all, and what is worse, I can't see any way of remedying the situation."

"I don't think any of us can do anything," Ellen said. "We'll just have to go on as we have been."

"Perhaps for the present we will," T. F. said. "But I'll not let the matter drop. I will not, however, take any steps just now."

We sat in silence for a few minutes, and then I nodded to Ellen. "I'm glad you are out of there, little sister," I said. "I shall stay until I can afford to marry Bettina, but it's not a pleasant house to live in right now. Yes, you and Jay are well out of it—by the way, do you hear from him?"

"I almost forgot!" she exclaimed, and jumping up she went over to an escritoire in the corner of the room and opened one of its drawers. "I had this letter last week. He sent it to me in care of Margit van Eyck. Read it, Robert, while I see about tea."

Jay was in Boston, working in a hospital while studying to become a doctor. "You have no idea, Ellen," he wrote, "how exhilarating life outside the bounds of parental jurisdiction has proved to be."

Even though I work until I am ready to drop—which I cannot afford to do, since I still have studying to get through at day's end—I am entirely happy, and completely confident that I have put myself on the right path.

Please assure Mama that I am in good health and spirits, but you'd better not mention my name to Papa (you know why). What did he say when he discovered the Ship's Clock was gone? I would have loved to have seen his face.

Write to me in care of the above address. I long to hear from you.

Your soon-to-be-a-doctor brother,
Jay

P.S. The Ship's Clock is in a safe place.

"What does he mean by 'you know why'?" I asked Ellen when she returned to the parlor.

"He and Papa had a violent disagreement the night of the fire," she answered thoughtfully. "Perhaps some day Jay will tell you about it; I cannot. But I will say this: Had I been in his place, I would have left home."

A young Irish maid appeared with the tea tray at that point, and the conversation turned to current topics: the rapid rebuilding of Wall Street, the cost of the fire damage, and the general economic picture.

"I do not think the future of the financial world is as auspicious as it might be," T. F. said, accepting the cup Ellen handed him. "Word is out that the number of nonguaranteed loans is too high. We might be headed for a panic—what do you hear at the bank, Robert?"

"Much the same thing, sir. But the City National has always been a conservative institution and will continue to be so, I am sure. I don't see that they're anticipating any losses at the moment."

"Willebrandt and Pyne is handling a couple of things for your bank, Robert," Ian said. "One interesting case I've been working on concerns the possible invasion of a trust by the legatee. Mr. Pyne's in charge of it, of course, but he has so much else pending that he's giving me almost a free hand."

Ian's going to make a success of the law, I thought, watching Ellen's interested expression as he related some of the details of the case. And Jay will be a great doctor. And I will be a rich banker. And our father will be left out of our lives.

Before I left we agreed that it would be safe for Ellen to visit Mama during the day when Papa would be at the shop, and that I should come to Stuyvesant Square as often as possible. This arrangement seemed to be as close as we could come to a reconciliation between the two Ferguson families, and while it was far from satisfactory it did prevent complete estrangement.

"Copy down this address, and write to Jay from the bank," Ellen said as I stood up to go. "It's plain that he does not want to lose touch with us."

I did as she asked, and Jay replied almost immediately. I continued to write to him at fairly regular intervals, and after a while I began to feel that I was closer to him at a distance than I had been during all the years we shared a room. Maturity, perhaps.

Ellen	I made a point of going to see my mother in the mornings when Paul and Annetta were at school. It wasn't that I didn't want to see those two—I longed to spend some time with them—but I was afraid they were too young to be trusted not to make some reference to my visit, even a word or two, that Papa might overhear. What a sorry state of affairs! I hated the feeling that we were all hiding things; even Mama seemed to be less open than usual. I soon refrained from asking her how Papa fared, because the only answer she ever

gave me was "he keeps going," which was no answer at all.

In the meantime my life with Ian was pure delight. As T. F. had said to Robert, we had the house on Stuyvesant Square to ourselves most of the time, and thanks to T. F.'s generosity there was plenty of money for our needs and for whatever entertainment we fancied. Aside from an occasional dinner at the newly opened Astor House, though, we seldom went out in the evening, preferring to retire early to our huge four-poster bed with its crimson canopy and hangings. Not surprisingly, I soon became pregnant, and could not have gone out in society in any case.

Ian, and T. F. when he was home, hovered over me as if I were a fragile flower, making Mama laugh at their nervous fussing whenever she came to call on me. I sailed through the nine months with a minimum of discomfort, and when our son Philip Andrew was born in January 1837, I wrote to Papa, thinking he might be pleased to hear that he had a grandson. He wasn't, though. Mama told me he read my letter quickly and then tore it to shreds.

"He did not speak to anyone for the rest of the evening," she reported, "so you can see that your kind gesture was wasted. But do not trouble yourself, Liebchen; you know as well as I do that Papa is not the man he used to be." She paused for a moment, and when she went on, the wistful note in her voice was unmistakable. "Nor is he the man who courted me long ago."

She sighed, and looked down at the sleeping baby on her lap. "Tell me, Ellen, what made you choose Philip for his name?"

"It's the name of Ian's closest friend in Australia," I answered, "and I liked the sound of Philip Ferguson. But Mama, what *was* Papa like when you first knew him? To me he has always been someone I had to be careful not to make cross. Oh, he could be good company, I know, and I think he really cared for us when we were children. He would play games with us in the evening, and sometimes he'd take Robert and Jay and me on board one of the ships on a Sunday afternoon. But we we were always a bit fearful, at least Jay and I were, and perhaps Robert was as well, of making a misstep, doing something that would displease him. You were the only one he never scolded, you know."

"Yes," she said slowly, "he was happier in those days, and he tried to be a good father, Liebchen. I know he tried. But you must remember that he always had things on his mind. Coming to America and starting a new life here as he did was not easy, and he was always striving to make a success of himself. He did, too, and for many years—up until the time Paul was born—things went well, and he made me happy. But now . . ."

"What happened, Mama? I know about the loss of the *Seagull*, but he made good after that, and moved us out of Maiden Lane. He seemed happy when we first lived in 233, too. Of course he had that awful injury to his leg, but he began to change before that. I think it was after T. F. called looking for his brother. Yes, it was then that he forbade Jay and Robert to have anything to do with T. F. or Ian—that was when he really became unreasonable. What on earth did they ever do to him? Why won't he see them? Why is he so against them?"

My mother shook her head, and did not answer me right away.

"I cannot say," she said finally. "No, I cannot—oh, look, your little one is waking up. Is it not time to feed him?"

I thought it best not to press her further, but as I sat nursing my baby I wondered if she meant she was unable to answer my questions, or whether she chose to keep the answers to herself.

The financial panic that T. F. had predicted struck the city in March of that year. Hundreds of firms went bankrupt, banks stopped payments, and thousands of people were suddenly unemployed. Mama told me that Mr. Hone, our neighbor, was hurt badly. He was in the process of building a new house on Great Jones Street when his oldest son's firm, Brown and Hone, stopped payments to its creditors, and since Mr. Hone had endorsed their bills he was liable for large amounts that he could ill afford at the time.

Papa's shop did not fail, but it "went to the brink," as Robert put it. He kept out of debt, but there was so little money coming in that he was forced to give up the house on

Broadway and move Mama, Annetta, and Paul to a small wooden structure on Warren Street, where the rents were cheap. I hoped it wouldn't catch fire; 233 Broadway was a stone house with a slate roof, as required by law for any building of more than two stories, and we never feared fire there. Robert, who had sustained only minor losses during the panic, was told to find his own accommodations.

"I was just as glad to get out, Ellen," my brother said, "but I didn't relish being pushed out that way. I've taken a room at Mrs. Howe's boarding house; it's reasonable, and will do for the present."

I could have invited him to stay with us, I suppose. I knew that Ian and T. F. would not have objected, and there was an extra bedroom on the third floor, but I did not want to relinquish the lovely long spells of privacy I had with Ian when T. F. was away. I felt guilty for a while, but when I saw how Robert enjoyed being what he called "a free agent," I consoled myself with the thought that he might have felt it necessary to conform to our habits and schedules, whether he liked it or not. When I wrote to Jay about this, his advice was brief: "Don't be silly, Ellen. Enjoy yourself."

James

I had never doubted that my decision to leave home the night of the Great Fire was the right one, and when I read Ellen's and Robert's accounts of the events that took place after my departure I was doubly glad to be on my own. It wasn't easy at first, but I was too determined to reach my goal and become a physician to let discomfort, even hunger, interfere with my entrance into what I considered the noblest of professions.

I had only sixty-two dollars and a few cents to my name when I stole out of the house with the Ship's Clock carefully stowed away in my satchel, bent on making my way to Boston. I could have stayed in the city and applied at New York Hospital, but I did not want to risk running into my father. Besides, I liked what I'd heard about Massachusetts General.

Leaning into an icy wind that blew off the East River, I hurried down to the docks on South Street, where I hoped to find inexpensive accommodations on a boat bound for Boston. I made inquiries at several of the packets and cargo ships tied up opposite the shops of the chandlers and offices of the shipping merchants. Only one, the *Mary B.,* carrying a shipment of cotton, was scheduled to sail the next day, but she had no provision for passengers. Not a little discouraged, I sat down in a darkened doorway to rest and to think, first arming myself with a discarded capstan spar to ward off any stray river rats.

Except for an occasional sailor making his unsteady way back to his ship, South Street was empty at that hour, and in the relative quiet, broken only by the creaking of the ships at their moorings, I dozed off. It was still dark when I was startled awake by shouts and sounds of scuffling somewhere close by. I stood up, and in the dim light I could just make out three figures pummeling one another not twenty feet away from me. As I watched, one of them was knocked to the ground, and a moment later the other two were on him.

By the time I covered the short distance between us the man who had fallen was thrashing about, trying desperately to break the hold the other two had on him. Since no one had seen me coming I caught the assailants unprepared. The first one howled when I brought the capstan spar down on his shoulders, and when his companion turned to see what had happened, I grabbed him by the collar and pulled him off his prey. Moments later it was all over: The victim scrambled to his feet, and between us we dealt his attackers a series of such punishing blows that they took to their heels and disappeared into the darkness of Jones Lane.

"Glad you showed up when you did, son," gasped the man I had rescued. "Those hoodlums would have taken every cent of my pay, and—"

"Are you all right, sir?" I could see by his uniform that he was no ordinary sailor.

91

"A bit bruised and sore in the head from falling on the cobblestones, but nothing serious. How did you happen along at this hour, anyway?"

After I had explained my situation (without going into the reasons for my leaving home) he looked me up and down carefully before speaking.

"I am in your debt, young man," he said after a moment or two, "and I should like to repay you. As it happens, the cook's boy has had an accident—broke his leg—and we could use another hand in the galley. Perhaps—"

"Are you—" I began.

"I'm Coates, first mate on the *Mary B*. What do you say? I'll give you passage to Boston if you fill in for Busby. No experience necessary; just do whatever Cookie tells you."

In no time at all I had collected my satchel and followed Mr. Coates aboard the *Mary B.*, feeling almost grateful to the two hoodlums.

I'd rather walk from New York to Boston than make that trip again. I don't even want to think about it. When I took leave of the *Mary B*. late in the afternoon two days later, I was not only dirty and unshaven, but I also smelled of fried fish and cooking grease. Had it been summertime I think I would have immersed myself fully clothed in the cleansing waters of Boston Harbor. Instead I buried my chin in the collar of my greatcoat and set out to find a rooming house, cheered by the thought that my small hoard of money was still intact.

I'd had next to no sleep on the voyage, so after a thorough wash and a quick meal I went early to bed in a cold box of a room on the top floor of a nondescript house overlooking Boylston Street. Anxious to make a start on my career, I left shortly before eight o'clock the next morning after obtaining directions to North Allen street, where Massachusetts General was located. I saw my fellow boarders exchange puzzled glances when I asked where the hospital was, and noticed that they kept their distance from me thereafter. It occurred to me later that they thought I was sick, possibly carrying some infectious disease.

I guess I did not look too healthy, because when I first presented myself at the hospital I was taken for a patient. When I protested that I was quite well, and that I wished to study medicine, I was shown into the office of a Dr. Rogers, one of the attending physicians, who explained the system to me.

"You can start by apprenticing yourself to one of the resident doctors—if you can find one who will have you—and by attending Harvard's three-month course of lectures. They are given every winter. In the meantime, how do you propose to support yourself?"

When I replied that I would do any kind of work connected with medicine, he offered me a position as an attendant (not to be confused with the attending physician), a helper in the wards.

"You will live at the hospital, eat and sleep here," he said, watching my face for any reaction, "and you will be at the beck and call of the house physicians, ready to carry out any orders they give you. Keep your eyes and ears open, and you'll absorb more clinical knowledge than you'll ever get from books and lectures. The work you will do will undoubtedly seem menial to you, and you may find that you haven't the stomach for medicine after all."

"I do not think that will be the case, sir," I responded, conscious of the searching look he turned on me. "My stomach is a strong one, and even if it weren't I should not let it interfere with my desire to become a physician."

He smiled, as if he'd heard all that before. "I'll turn you over to Old George now. He's been an attendant here for years; he came in as a charity patient, and never wanted to leave. He'll show you the ropes."

———

93

Everything Dr. Rogers said to me proved to be true. As I watched the house physicians and the residents at work and listened to their comments, I soaked up clinical knowledge like a sponge. Naturally I made every effort to spend as much time in their company as possible, but the menial jobs were ever present and never ending. I emptied slops, cleaned up vomit, changed bloody bandages, kept patients from lying in their own filth, broke up fights in the wards, and learned how to take abuse, especially from alcoholics, who blamed me for curtailing their supply of spirits. A harder lesson to learn was that I could not afford to let my heart break when a pain-wracked patient begged me for opium, or a sick and frightened child clung to me, crying piteously. One little boy with a badly fractured leg reminded me of Paul . . .

Fortunately I was too physically exhausted at the end of the day to stay awake long enough to let my mind dwell on the tragic cases I had seen during working hours. No matter how late it was, though, when I climbed the long flights of stairs to the dismal quarters provided for the attendants, I performed two tasks without fail, a nightly ritual: I washed myself thoroughly from head to foot (often in ice cold water), and I made sure the Ship's Clock was safe in its hiding place, unwound and silent. Thievery was not uncommon among the poorly paid helpers.

I had pried up a floorboard in one corner of the cubicle assigned to me and found a space just large enough to accommodate the clock. Then I replaced the board, and moved my cot over it. The Ship's Clock did present a problem, and at first I did not stop to analyze my reasons for guarding it so carefully, but later on I gave the matter some thought. It occurred to me that I was responsible for an object considered to be a family treasure, albeit a treasure wrongfully in my possession. To my father the Ship's Clock represented what amounted to an almost sacred trust: the continuity of the family line over the centuries. At least that is what I understood him to mean one Sunday noontime years ago when he was holding forth on the intricate workmanship of the clock after it had struck the hour. He ended up with what almost sounded like a prayer:

"Father to son, father to son," he intoned, "from the patriarch of one generation to his successor in the next, and so on and on, until time runs out. That has been the tradition, and I shall see that it continues. Robert, you must prove yourself worthy to be its owner and protector, and then your son . . ."

I must see that Robert does have it, I thought, but not now. Suddenly I began to wish I had not taken it; anger at my father, as well as desire for revenge of some sort had prompted me to steal it, but now that I had it, what was I to do with it? I could neither part with it nor set it going for my own amusement, nor could I display it to my co-workers. So it remained concealed, more of a burden than anything else.

Almost a year elapsed before I began to question the wisdom of my decision to become a doctor, not because I was bored with the work, but because it occurred to me that I might, like Old George, remain an attendant for the rest of my life. My inquiries concerning an apprenticeship had produced no encouraging replies, and I was on the verge of returning to New York to take my chances at Bellevue when I met Caroline Hagedorn.

I almost stumbled over her: I had been ordered to escort a mentally disturbed patient to McLean Hospital, where the facilities for dealing with the deranged were better than ours, and was on my way back to North Allen Street when I saw her. Even though the December afternoon was cold and gray, I was glad to be outdoors, away from the wards, and was walking slowly, deep in thought about my future, when my foot struck her small boot.

At first I took her for a woman of the streets—there were many of them in that area—who had collapsed either from hunger or from overindulgence in spirits. She lay against an iron railing, her skirts awry, and her bonnet pulled down in such a way as to conceal her face. One arm was flung out, with the fingers of the open hand slightly curving inward, ready to close around alms from a passerby.

I spoke to her, and when she failed to respond I knelt down and pushed the bonnet aside to see if she were alive. The beauty of the pale, heart-shaped face thus revealed made me gasp, a beauty unmarred by the blood that had matted her dark hair and trickled down over the right side of her forehead.

No streetwalker, she, I thought as I examined her delicate features and took note of the expensive quality of the fur-trimmed cloak she wore. When I ascertained that her pulse was extremely shallow, I wasted no more time. I picked her up as gently as I could, careful to rest the left side of her head against my shoulder so as not to start the bleeding again, and carried her the short distance into the hospital.

She hovered between life and death for the rest of the day, and I visited the ward in which she had been placed as often as I could.

"In love, are you, Jamie?" Old George asked quietly when he saw me gazing down at her.

"Just wondering if she's going to live," I mumbled, turning away in embarrassment. "That's all." I wasn't in love then; interested was more like it.

I was glad I made one last visit to the ward before going up to bed that night, since she regained consciousness while I was standing at her bedside.

"It's all right; you're safe here," I said in answer to the frightened inquiry in her dark blue eyes. "I found you lying on the street, and brought you into the hospital. You're going to be fine."

"They pulled my reticule from my wrist," she whispered, "and I think I fell when one of them pushed me."

"You must have hit your head on the railing when you

went down," I said. "You were unconscious when I came along. But the wound is slight, and will heal—"

"Who are you?" she interrupted. "I am in your debt, and would like to repay your kindness."

"Nonsense!" I said briskly. "I just happened to be there—"

"I know you are a doctor, but what is your name?" she persisted.

"James Ferguson," I replied, "and I am still struggling to become a doctor."

"I am Caroline Hagedorn," she said with a warm smile, "and I am very pleased to make your acquaintance, James Ferguson. Would you be so kind as to have someone notify my parents that I am here? They will be worried to death."

"A fine feather in your cap, Jamie," Dr. Rogers said to me the next day, after Miss Hagedorn had been transferred to a private room. "She is the only daughter of Charles Lewis Hagedorn, and the apple of his eye. He was beside himself with worry about her—you know who he is, don't you? No? None other than the respected and admired head of the trustees of the hospital. A most important and influential personage. No doubt he'll want to thank you personally for what you did."

My rescue of Caroline Hagedorn marked a turning point in both my private and professional lives. I found myself devising ways of slipping off to the private wing to look at the lovely patient in the flower-filled room on the floor above the wards. I never could stay long, but even a few minutes in her company would send my spirits soaring. They would quickly plummet, though, when I remembered that she'd return home soon, leaving me nothing but the memory of her beauty.

My mood was as somber as the sunless December morning when Mr. Hagedorn sent word that he would like to see me in his office next to the boardroom at three o'clock that afternoon. I expected no more than a pat on the back, a friendly handshake, or a few words of thanks, but Mr. Hagedorn had more than that in mind.

I had pictured the head of the board of trustees as a tall, austere man, of military bearing, someone who expected to be obeyed without question, and was surprised to be greeted cordially by a short, rather plump gentleman with red cheeks and friendly blue eyes. His very appearance put me at my ease.

As we sat in the elegant gloom of his richly furnished office he began, not by thanking me, but by questioning me closely about my education and my plans for the future.

"I was within a few months of graduating from Columbia College," I said slowly, "when my father needed me to help him out in his business, so I was forced to leave school. Later, when things improved, I felt free to strike out on my own, to pursue my chosen career." I had no wish to reveal the sordid side of my departure from New York.

"And you have been an attendant for about a year, now?" he asked.

"Yes, sir. I've been unable to find an opening for an apprenticeship."

"That will be remedied," he said briskly. "You have done me a great service, James, and Caroline's mother and I wish to express our gratitude. Also, the reports I've received of your work here are extremely good."

He paused, stared at me for a moment, and then smiled as he stood up.

"Off you go, young man," he said, extending his hand. "You will hear from one of the house physicians. God be with you."

He was as good as his word: He saw to it that I was apprenticed to Dr. Richard Douglaston, and arranged matters so that I could attend the mandatory three months of lectures at Harvard. He also took a personal interest in my progress, and from time to time had me report to him, either in the office in which I had first seen him, or in his own home.

My visits to his house on Chestnut Street generally took place in the evening, and each time I approached the handsome, four-story building with its columned doorway and wrought iron balconies I experienced a pleasurable sense of excitement. After my conference with Mr. Hagedorn in his library we would join Caroline and her mother in the green and gold drawing room for refreshments. Mrs. Hagedorn, a small, bright-eyed, cheerful woman, was convinced that the hospital half-starved its employees, and made a point of plying me with hearty sandwiches and cakes "made with plenty of the best butter and eggs."

"Young James will have to be measured for a new set of clothes if you keep this up, my love," her husband said one evening in the spring.

"Indeed not, Charles," she retorted. "He's thin as a rail from being run off his feet. And see how he relishes those cream cakes! I can tell he's underfed."

Dr. Hagedorn sighed, his wife passed the plate of fancy cakes again, and Caroline smiled across at me. I remember that she looked particularly beautiful that evening in some sort of flowered gown with ruffles of lace at her wrists and at her throat. It was difficult, as it so often was, to keep my gaze from lingering on her too long.

As the months went on I began to call more and more frequently at the Hagedorn mansion, as often as I could spare time from my duties at the hospital. My pleasure in those visits was marred only on the occasions when Caroline was not present. At first I inquired about her absence, but upon being told that she was at this or that ball or cotillion I experienced such pangs of jealousy that I asked no further questions. Perhaps I was still only infatuated, but I thought of myself as being deeply in love. As I walked back to the hospital after an evening spent with the senior Hagedorns in what seemed like an empty drawing room, I tried to console myself by picturing her escort as a short, fat fellow with a snout for a nose, or else an awkward gangling scarecrow with no hair on his head. Not that that helped very much.

I knew I was in no position to compete with the sons of the wealthy families in the Hagedorn circle, but I also knew that Caroline had done nothing to discourage my suit. On the contrary, she seemed to give little signals that she looked upon me favorably; on warm evenings when the two of us strolled in the walled garden alongside the house she would take my arm, and once or twice I thought I detected a slight extra pressure from her small hand. She appeared to be completely at ease in my company, chattering away about the events of her day, asking me about my family life in New York, and listening carefully to my replies.

I yearned to take her in my arms, to hold her, feel her lips on mine, and to ask her to wait for me to become established in private practice, but something—fear of being refused, I suppose—made me hold back. I continued to dream, however.

By the spring of 1840 I had completed my medical studies, passed the necessary examinations, and could at last affix the coveted M.D. to my name. I was ready to speak to Dr. Hagedorn, to ask his permission to marry Caroline as soon as I could support her, when the blow fell. On the fifteenth of April her engagement to Harley Sedgwick, son of Mr. and Mrs. Everett Sedgwick of 10 Walnut Street, was announced. The wedding would take place in June.

For the second time in my life I thought I might die of a broken heart, and for the second time I recovered nicely, helped no doubt by the unexpected (and welcome) appearance of my old classmate and stage door friend, Dan Jennings. He had completed his training at Bellevue and was in Boston to study the treatment of mental patients at McLean Hospital. I'd always enjoyed his company, and when he asked me to share the flat he'd rented I accepted with alacrity. Thanks to him and my natural recuperative powers, my last months at Massachusetts General were not spent in mourning a lost love.

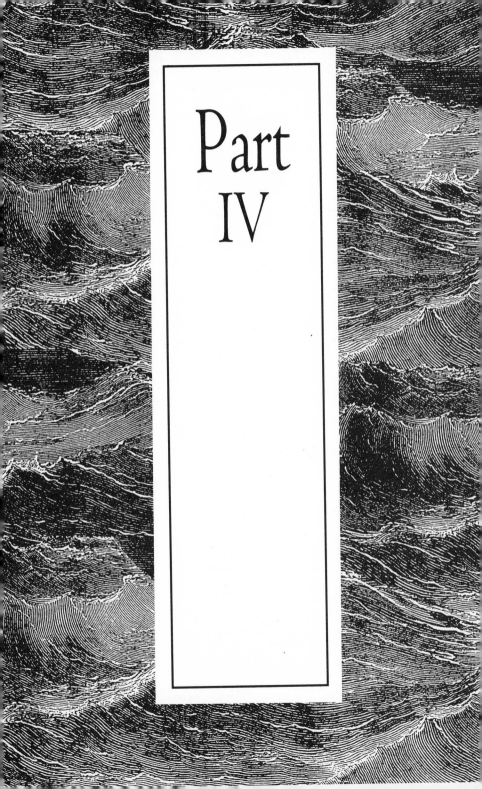

Part
IV

Ellen

During the 1840s I was so wrapped up in my family life that I paid little attention to what was going on in the outside world. One pregnancy after another followed in rapid succession, and by the end of the decade I had produced three more sons and one daughter, besides suffering through two miscarriages. With so many children we needed more room than T. F.'s house afforded, and in 1846 we moved to a large town house on Washington Square North, a lovely quiet section of the city. T. F. established himself in a set of rooms at the Clarendon Residential Hotel on Fourth Avenue and Eighteenth Street, saying that although he loved his grandchildren dearly he needed peace and quiet in his advancing years. He was sixty-four then but looked and acted like a man in his late forties.

The years had not been as kind to my own father; he looked far older than sixty-five, with his bent figure, sparse gray hair, and deeply lined face. Decrepit, that's the word I want. He had, however, mellowed to the point where he permitted me to visit Mama, but he would still have nothing to do with T. F. or Ian, or even allow their names to be mentioned in his presence.

After selling the Maiden Lane property together with the business (for a handsome sum, according to Robert), Papa bought a rather attractive house on Henry Street, the back parlor of which he converted into a bedroom for himself so that he would no longer have to climb the stairs. His bad leg may have forced him to live on one floor, but it did not prevent him from going out when it suited him to do so.

"I do not know where he goes," my mother complained. "Some days he is gone for hours, sometimes in a carriage, and sometimes on foot, hobbling along. And he will not answer my questions. What can he be doing? Other days he sits looking out the window, as if waiting for someone to ring the doorbell. Then at night he goes back into his bedroom. Some days he hardly says two words to me, but several times lately I've heard him talking to himself, not loud enough for me to understand, though. I worry about his mind now, and I know his leg troubles him more and more, too, but he will have nothing to do with doctors. Oh, if he would only let James examine him!"

Jay had returned from Boston in the early forties, and worked for a few years at Bellevue Hospital before going into private practice, where he was enormously successful. His good looks, his gentle manner, and his professional skill had patients clamoring for his services.

"James should marry," Mama said. "At thirty-five a man should have a wife and children. Thank goodness Bettina waited for Robert—how can it be that they are still childless? I don't know what took Robert so long; money, I suppose. Paul at twenty is still too young, and too busy learning to be an architect—oh, and look at Annetta! Such a hasty marriage! It grieved your father."

She sighed and shook her head ruefully. Annetta's marriage to a young artist had been one more bitter pill for Papa to swallow. If ever he had loved anyone aside from Mama it was my younger sister. She'd been winsomely pretty as a child, charming as a young girl, and incredibly lovely as a grown woman. No wonder Papa adored her; everyone did.

She was twenty-two when she married Pierre Du Champs. Contrary to my mother's belief it was not a marriage made in haste, but Mama couldn't have known that. Pierre had been to the house on Henry Street only once, and on that occasion my father had received him so coldly that the visit was not repeated.

"What am I going to do, Ellen?" Annetta wailed after telling me how Papa had behaved. "Pierre is a gentleman, an artist, what will he think of me, of my family? He says Papa's attitude makes no difference, but I'm afraid—"

"Afraid he'll think less of you? I doubt that," I said. "Perhaps if you brought him here—yes, come for supper on Sunday. I'd like to meet him. And then we'll see what can be done."

The worried look vanished from her face, and she flung her arms around me the way she did when she was little. "I knew you'd help me! Oh, Ellen, what would I do without you? Pierre means so much to me—oh, you'll like him, Ellen!"

I did like the handsome, well-dressed, serious young man who appeared with a smiling Annetta late on Sunday afternoon. When she said he was an artist I had a vision of a poverty-stricken youth painting away in a dusty garret, but I was completely, utterly wrong.

"Oh, yes, I do paint," Pierre said in response to a question of Ian's, "but I am here in your country to acquire samples of American art. I have bought some of William Prior's portraits of children that are most charming and unusual, and am negotiating for samples of the Hudson River School—landscapes, you know. You see, my family owns a gallery in Paris, and in a few years I shall be managing it. My father wishes to devote his remaining years to his vineyards in the Loire Valley."

"I have visited the Du Champs gallery," T. F. said, advancing to shake Pierre's hand, "and very impressive it is, too."

Thank heavens he's not a penniless painter, I thought, glancing at Annetta's pleased expression before turning to lead the way into the dining room.

"Annetta has chosen well," Ian said after the guests departed. "I hope we'll see more of that young man. I found him most interesting."

"We will," I said, slipping my arm through his as we mounted the stairs. "I promised Annetta she could bring him here any time. I'll try to arrange to let them have some privacy—perhaps the back parlor . . ."

Ian laughed and hugged me. "That's something you and I had little enough of, isn't it, dearest? But look what we have now!" With that he guided me into the bedroom and locked the door.

"Why are you smiling, Liebchen?" Mama's voice brought me back to the present. "Annetta could have had the pick of New York society, and look who she chose! Ah, well, when one is in love one is not always able to reason clearly. You have been most fortunate, Ellen, but if I were you I would not have any more babies. Five is enough, and you are not as young as you once were. Do not sleep with Ian for a while. Oh, I know it will be hard—just wait until you go through the change, then you can do whatever pleases you."

She may have guessed how worried I was when I was carrying Fanny; Will, our fourth son, had been born with a club foot, and throughout my fifth pregnancy I was haunted by fears of an even worse deformity in my baby. No, those nine months had not been tranquil, and while I did not relish the thought of still another pregnancy, neither did I like the prospect of many celibate years. I was only thirty-four when this conversation took place and loath to turn away from Ian's tender, wonderful lovemaking, an act that would distress him as much as it would me. No, I would not, absolutely would not give up our nights of passion, I thought, come what may. Then suddenly the matter was taken out of my hands.

Ian had long since been made a partner in the firm of Willebrant and Pyne, and although most of his work dealt with wills, trusts, and estates, he was ready at all times to accept cases involving social justice. He felt strongly about the plight of the runaway slaves, who passed through New York by the hundreds on their way to Canada. Those were the lucky ones; the unfortunate ones were apprehended and returned to their southern owners. Ian and his friend John Jay, a grandson of the first chief justice of the United States Supreme Court, were active in the New York Young Men's Antislavery Society, and both were more than willing to defend escaped slaves in court. I thought Ian was involving himself in a dangerous business, since it was a federal offense to refuse to aid an agent in the capture of such a slave, and said as much.

"I have nothing to do with the capturing," he argued when I expressed my concern, "and everything to do with the release. No man can accuse me of breaking the law on that count."

And yet someone did—did far worse than that. Late on a rainy afternoon in November 1850, my husband was found lying in a dark doorway near the Tombs Prison, where he had gone to interview an escapee prior to a court appearance. A passerby saw him and called the police, and Ian was carried into our house in much the same manner in which my father had been borne home years before.

He had been brutally beaten about the head and lay in a coma for three days. Jay did everything he could, bringing in colleagues and trying various remedies, but to no avail. Ian died at four o'clock in the morning of November twelfth. His assailant was not found. A vagrant who had been sifting through the rubbish at the end of an alley had seen a man who was leaning on a cane disappearing up the street shortly before the passerby stopped to help Ian, but he had not seen the attack itself.

"The man with the cane could have done it, Ellen," John Jay said to me later, "but the vagrant is an old bum, and had been drinking that day, so no one gives much credence to what he says. The authorities are agreed that everything points to Ian's being set upon by a thug, or thugs, hired by a slave owner anxious to get his property back. I don't like it, but I'm afraid there's no chance of locating either the thug or the owner."

I could understand why no one wanted to believe the drunken vagrant, and I knew I was allowing my imagination to run wild, but when a cane was mentioned I felt my heart lurch. I had seen my father raise his cane, and my brother Jay's description of how he had beaten the looters the night of the fire sprang to mind. I said nothing to anyone about my suspicion, but I could not banish the thought from my mind that Ian could have been struck with the brass knob that served as a handle on my father's ebony stick.

Was it possible that he hated Ian enough to do that? To kill my husband, my lover, my true love?

The terrible, deep despair that threatened to encompass me had to be pushed away while I dealt with the problems of everyday living. I know now that it was a good thing that I *had* those problems, but at the time I resented them, and wanted only to sit quietly and give myself up to grief. But what mother can do that when young children are in need of attention?

If it had not been for T. F.'s generous help I could not have supported my family. We had lived up to Ian's income, and while I never felt we were extravagant, I know we didn't stint ourselves on items such as food, clothing, domestic help, and the like. With his death I found myself with virtually nothing; the dividends that came at intervals from the few shares of railroad stock Ian had bought at Robert's urging would not have kept my household running even if I economized drastically. T. F. was adamant about my accepting his help and brushed off my protests impatiently.

"It will all come to you and the young ones in the end, my dear Ellen," he said, "and I couldn't live with myself if I knew you and my grandchildren were having to do without."

"I don't know how I can ever thank you enough," I said tearfully as I searched for a handkerchief.

"Well, you can," he said, "just by allowing me to do it, and permitting me to come visit you. I like the idea of keeping an eye on the next generation of Fergusons. It will take my mind off the past . . ."

He did come, too, and much more frequently than he had when Ian was alive. He genuinely loved the children, and while he played no favorites, I think what delighted him most was the endearing way two-year-old Fanny held out her arms to him to be picked up even before he had taken off his hat and coat. I can still picture him sitting in the large wing chair, looking down at her on his lap as she played with his heavy gold watch chain.

Amongst the children, Fanny alone was unaffected by Ian's death. Philip, I believe, felt it more deeply than Rodney or John or William, although from time to time one of the younger ones would ask plaintively why Pa had to die, but their grief could not compare with Philip's or mine.

Now that I think of it, it was easy enough to get through the day, but during the long hours of the night, when sleep was elusive, my yearning for Ian's presence was almost unbearable. I remember moving over to his side of our large bed, pretending my head was on his shoulder, and that in a few minutes I'd feel his hand on by breast, his lips on mine. Then tears of sorrow, rage, frustration—I don't know which—would follow, to continue until finally, long after midnight, I would fall asleep, exhausted, unhappy, and unfulfilled.

Jay must have had some idea of what I was going through, because he prescribed a mild sleeping draught for me, and advised me to take a glass of claret with my evening meal. He made a point of dropping in on us several times a week, sometimes for only a few minutes, but often for a quiet hour with me by the fire after the children were in bed. His presence was comforting in that I was under no pressure to pretend that all was well, as I had to do when T. F. or Mama came. He laughed when I told him she was upset that he hadn't married, and said he was in no hurry. "I'll probably marry some day, Ellen, but not immediately. I've been thinking about it, but—oh, tell Mama I have no intention of remaining a bachelor forever. By the way, does she ever ask you about the Ship's Clock? She never says anything to me."

"Where is it, Jay?"

"In a safe place. Would you like to have it here? You could put it up there on the mantel. It might amuse the children."

"Oh, I don't know, Jay."

"There's no danger of Papa's seeing it, if that's what's on your mind."

"No, I know that, but I really don't want it. I think you'd better keep it."

"I wonder," he said musingly after a moment or two, "why Papa set such store by it. I know it's old, and probably has some value as an antique, but it's certainly not worth a fortune. It must have some special meaning for him, some association, other than just having been in the family for generations. Remember how he used to let us watch it on special occasions when we were small?" He smiled at the recollection.

"Yes, and do you remember how fascinated Cousin Hans was when he came to visit? Something about the way he acted made me think he was familiar with it."

112

"Cousin Hans Mesner! Yes, I do remember that, Ellen. But he spent all his time talking to Mama in German, so we never knew what he said about it."

"Well," I said when he paused, "what are you going to do with it?"

"Leave it where it is, I suppose," he shrugged, "locked up in a cabinet in my office. You're sure you won't take it?"

"Positive. But, you know, Jay, you could always give it back to Papa—"

"Never!" he exclaimed. "I told you what he did to me, didn't I? The reason I took it?"

"Yes, you did, and you also wrote to me about it."

"Well, then—"

No more was said about the Ship's Clock that night, but a few days later Jay surprised me by saying he had put it on display in his office.

"It's amazing, Ellen, how it captures the interest of all but the dullest patients—I mean the ones who can't see or hear very well. The others are enchanted by it. One elderly man even asked me if he could bring his young grandson in to see it, and I can't tell you how many times I've seen the face of a patient, even one in pain, light up when the clock performs. You might bring the children someday—not all five at once, though."

I laughed and said I would try to arrange a series of visits.

"Speaking of arranging things, my dear sister, would you feel up to giving a small dinner party for me? You see, I am indebted to a few people, and other than taking them out to a hotel or a restaurant—and I don't want to do that—I have no way of repaying their hospitality. You know what my rooms are like."

Although he didn't come right out and say it, I was pretty sure Jay thought it would do me good to see some new faces, to have some interest besides my children, and in the end I was grateful, very grateful to him. By that time Ian had been dead for over a year, so society, if it took any notice of me at all, could not accuse me of coming out of mourning too soon. I went about making preparations for the dinner party as I had done so often when Ian was alive, planning the menu with Mrs. Billings, the cook, checking over the good silver, getting out the white china with the gold border, all the little things one does to get ready for even a minor social occasion. I had put all that aside for too long.

There were to be six of us at the table that snowy night shortly before Christmas; Dr. and Mrs. Middleton, Mr. and Mrs. Asbury, and my brother and I. The day before the party, however, Jay asked me if he could bring another friend along, a Dr. Jennings.

"You will like him, Ellen," he said. "I knew him first at Columbia, then I met up with him again in Boston, and now I see quite a bit of him here. Like us, he's the product of a German-Irish union—at least Papa is half Irish—but unlike us, he's fluent in German. His mother, a Schumann, saw to that, and apparently *his* father had no objection."

Of course I agreed to include Dr. Jennings, and even though the table was not properly balanced (seven is an awkward number to seat), everything went off smoothly, and I found that I was enjoying myself far more than I had anticipated. There were no mishaps in the kitchen, the roast was done perfectly, and Mrs. Billings outdid herself with the meringue glacé for dessert. And the company was good: The Middletons and Asburys were easygoing, pleasant conversationalists, obviously very fond of Jay. I liked them, but I was more interested in Daniel Jennings. He was quieter than the others, but when he did offer an observation or make a comment, it seemed to me that he cut right to the kernel of the discussion, causing one or more of us to say, "Ah, yes, that's it exactly." Also, I liked the way he inclined his head and listened attentively to whoever was speaking. Besides all this, he was strikingly handsome.

114

After the meal, while we were having coffee in the parlor, he admired a delicate blue-green Chinese jar that T. F. had picked up on his travels, and as I watched him bend over to examine it more closely I noted the gentleness with which his slender fingers traced the design.

"It's a beauty, Mrs. Ferguson," he said, straightening up and smiling at me, "and you've set it off to advantage on that little table against the dark paneling of the wall."

He laughed when I told him that ordinarily the jar was kept on a high shelf, out of reach of small, sticky fingers, and displayed only on special occasions. I was sorry that my attention was then called to one of the other guests, but was extraordinarily pleased that Dr. Jennings made an effort to draw me into conversation with him whenever the opportunity occurred.

"That was a wonderful party, Ellen," Jay said the next evening as he watched me embroider the face on a little rag doll I was making for Fanny's Christmas stocking. "I do thank you for having it. And, by the way, Jennings told me he'd enjoyed himself thoroughly."

"I'm glad to hear it, Jay," I said, looking up from my sewing. "I thought he was a bit quiet."

"He's been through a bad time; he hadn't been married very long when his wife became an invalid. She died about a year ago—consumption. He's very well off financially, though; his parents left him plenty."

"Are there any children?"

"No, she couldn't."

"No wonder he has a lonesome look."

"Yes, that's why I thought a bit of social life would do him good."

And that it would do me good, too, I thought. Well, it did do me good: the Asburys and the Middletons reciprocated with dinner invitations of their own, and on Christmas Eve a large box arrived from the florist with a note from Dr. Jennings asking if he might call on me the following Sunday. It's amazing what a little admiration and attention will do for a woman.

| James | Ellen's house on Washington Square gradually became the seat of our family gatherings, gatherings that should by tradition have taken place in our parents' home. Birthdays and holidays were celebrated by candlelight and firelight in her large dining room, and most of us were there for her informal Sunday night suppers. Robert, Bettina, and I were the regulars; Annetta appeared constantly, at least before she went off to Paris with her artist husband, and young Paul came whenever he could think of an excuse to escape from the |

Henry Street house.

"I feel as if I'm up a tree and can't get down, Jay," he said to me on one such occasion. "Papa thinks he has me all tied up because he's promised to leave me everything—(the rest of you have been disinherited, even Annetta)—if I stay living with him and Mama. That could be forever—until they die, I mean."

"Could you support yourself elsewhere?" I asked.

"Of course not. Not yet. I'm still working in Mr. Downing's office, learning to be an architect, not making enough to live on."

"Then I'd stay, if I were you, at least until you can open an office. If you're patient, and Papa leaves you his estate, you'll have some capital to start you off."

"I haven't much choice—I guess that's what I'll have to do. Actually it's not too bad, living there. I'm out most of the day, and studying upstairs at night. It's only when he gets in a temper about something that it's grim. When he does that, Mama goes up to her bedroom and locks the door until he quiets down. You never know what will set him off . . ."

I didn't like the sound of that; I'd seen how violent my father could become, and wondered if I shouldn't ask Paul to move in with me, into the empty room above my office. But that would mean that he'd be disinherited, too.

My thoughts were interrupted by T. F.'s arrival. He joined us frequently on Sundays, and as I watched him with Ellen's children, his face alight with tender affection, I could not help but shake my head at the difference between Ian's father and my own. How could this kind, gentle man pose a threat to Papa? Or to anyone, for that matter. I wondered if my father were demented, or if there was something in his past he did not want revealed and feared that T. F. might ferret it out. How wrong he was! T. F. was long gone when we learned the awful truth.

When I suggested to Ellen that she bring the young ones to my office to see the Ship's Clock, it never occurred to me that word of its presence would get back to its former owner. That's what happened, though, and not surprisingly the resultant uproar did nothing to heal the cleavage between me and my father.

On a warm, sunny afternoon in April Ellen arrived with the two younger boys, John and Will, who were about four and

118

six at the time, just the right age to be introduced to the little figures that marched across the deck when the clock struck. They were so taken with it that they insisted on returning an hour later to view the performance again. Ellen finally dragged them off, but only after promising to bring them back the following week.

I remember that I stood at the waiting room window for a minute or two, amused at the sight of the two small figures capering about my sister, Will still too young to be sensitive about the built-up shoe he was forced to wear. I smiled, happy for them, and happy for myself at the prospect of the evening that lay ahead. I was to spend it with Anne Everard . . .

I turned from the window, carried the Ship's Clock into the inner office, and placed it carefully in the back of a cupboard, behind my supply of pills and ointments. There had been a number of break-ins on Cortlandt Street recently, and while I was not overly concerned about becoming a victim of thieves, it occurred to me that the clock was easily visible to anyone passing by who happened to glance in the window of my waiting room.

I locked up the office, and taking the stairs two at a time, hurried into my bedroom to make ready for an evening devoted to pleasure. I had made Anne's acquaintance six months earlier when I was called in to attend her father, Bertrand Everard, a banker and financier who had never fully recovered from the losses he sustained in the panic of 1837. Whether it was worry over money matters or the pain caused by his gouty foot that affected Mr. Everard's disposition, I cannot say. In any event he was one of the most difficult, irascible, demanding, and unpleasant patients I have known to this day. Had it not been for Anne, whose unusual dark beauty and warm personality had enchanted me from the first, I would have long since turned him over to one of my younger colleagues, one with a fairly thick skin.

For her sake I continued to respond to his summons and to

do whatever possible to alleviate his physical discomfort, willingly suffering through a fifteen-minute tirade of complaint in order to spend a few minutes over a cup of tea with Anne downstairs in the parlor.

After only three or four visits of this sort I knew with complete certainty that I wanted her, wanted her more than I'd ever wanted anything or anyone in my life, and set about courting her in earnest. Neither she nor her mother did anything to discourage me, and if Mr. Everard had any inkling of my suit, he did not mention it.

It was late when I went to bed the night following Ellen's visit with the two boys. I had taken Anne to see a play at the Park Theater, at whose stage door I had waited with Jennings in so feverish a state for a glimpse of Fanny Kemble years ago. After the performance we lingered over a late supper at the Astor House, and I was further delayed by my inability to put an end to a number of prolonged embraces that took place in the privacy of the dimly lighted parlor of the Everard house.

It was after two o'clock before I fell asleep, only to be routed out of bed at dawn to deliver a carpenter's wife of twin boys. The rest of the day is a blur in my mind; I must have dealt with my patients, but all I remember clearly is locking up after the last one, putting the Ship's Clock in its cupboard, eating some bread and cheese and falling into bed at last.

I was awakened some twelve hours later by two things: the bright morning sun shining across my face (I had neglected to draw the curtains), and a loud rapping on the street door. I flung on my dressing gown and hurried down the steep staircase, thinking to see another frantic husband whose wife had gone into labor, only to be stunned by the sight of my father standing with his ever-present stick upraised, ready to bang on the door again. As I backed away, fearful that the blow would fall on my head or shoulders, he forced his way in, and brushing past me limped through the open door of my waiting room.

"Where is it?" he shouted. "The child said it was on the mantel in the front room! Speak up! Where have you hidden it? Tell me, or I shall have you arrested for a thief!"

"I knew at once what must have happened," I said to Ellen several days later when she and Robert and I were having tea in her parlor.

"Oh, Jay," she wailed, "he must have heard Will babbling away to Mama—you know how excited he was about seeing the clock! But what did you do?"

"I simply went into my office, took the clock out of the cupboard, and gave it to him. I was afraid he'd have a stroke if I didn't, and besides, I have a healthy respect for that stick of his."

"It was the only thing you could do, Jay," Robert said. "Otherwise—"

"Yes," Ellen interrupted, "and the clock is now where it belongs, but . . ." She frowned and studied her teacup before going on. "But I am surprised he came for it himself; he swore, you know, that he never would lay eyes on you again—and besides, his leg was paining him dreadfully when we were there."

"He was angry enough to do almost anything, Ellen," I said. "Rage has been known to give people strength they didn't know they had, even the strength to overlook pain."

"Surely he couldn't have walked all the way from Henry Street to your office, could he?" Robert asked.

"No, no. He had a carriage waiting outside. I saw it when he stomped out the door, the clock in one hand and the cane in the other. He looked terrible. His face is sunken because he's lost a number of teeth, and his breath is foul, but his limp didn't seem any worse that it was when we used to walk him down to the shop. If I were you though, Ellen, I wouldn't go visit Mama for a while. Let him simmer down. God, I hate to think of growing old like that."

"Don't think about it then," Robert said with a smile. "Here's some good news: Bettina and I are expecting a son and heir in December, in time for Christmas."

I took my leave shortly after Robert's happy announcement, saying I had promised to look in on a patient. In truth, I was anxious to catch up on sleep lost over the past two days and nights as a result of the Astor Place riots.

By an unfortunate coincidence Mr. William Macready, an English actor, was scheduled to appear at the Opera House in Astor Place in the role of Macbeth at the same time his American rival, Mr. Edwin Forrest, was playing the part farther downtown at the less opulent Broadway Theater. Probably nothing would have happened had not Ned Buntline, a fiery propagandist, incited the gangs of the notorious Five Points district with provocative broadsheets reading: "Do we want the English here? No! No! Send Macready home!" The Irish gang with which I had had some little contact as a boy had grown considerably in size (but not in wisdom) since the days of Rosie's back room, and it took little urging on Buntline's part to persuade them to join with other gangs in an effort to oust the Englishman.

When Macready appeared on the stage of the Opera House on the night of May seventh he was pelted with old shoes, rotten eggs, and various other missiles. The curtain came down, the performance was canceled, and the actor strode off, vowing never to set foot on that stage again. A group of prominent and influential New Yorkers, however, including the writer Washington Irving, persuaded him to reconsider, and on the night of May tenth Macready struggled to make himself heard over the hisses and catcalls from the audience.

Even though Dan Jennings and I had seats near the stage we had trouble hearing him.

He did finish the play in spite of the noise, and conscious of the increasing volume of the din outside the building, raced through the last two acts at top speed.

The mob outside the theater, not content with vocal protest, attacked the building itself, smashing doors and windows with brickbats and bludgeons in mounting hysteria, overpowering the police who had been sent to control them. The city militia was called out, and in an effort to stop the violence fired directly into the surging crowd. The carnage was hideous. Every available doctor, Jennings and I among them, worked steadily through the rest of the night and far into the next day, staunching wounds, setting bones, and doing what we could to ease the pain of the most seriously wounded—some of them, sadly, innocent bystanders.

I was tending a bullet wound in the chest of a big, burly fellow who lay on the pavement hardly breathing, when suddenly he opened his eyes and made an effort to speak. I thought he looked somewhat familiar, but it was not until he gasped, "Jamie—good boyo," that I recognized Randy O'Dair of the Kerryonian gang. A moment later he was gone, and I moved on to the next victim. O'Dair had hated the English to the end.

As I said, I was still feeling the effects of that experience a few days later at Ellen's, and as I walked home I could not but be grateful that she hadn't been at the Opera House that night, and that Jennings had gone with me when Anne found at the last minute that she was needed at home.

That summer was such a hot one that everyone who could afford it left the city. T. F. rented a large house in Rockaway for Ellen and the children, for all of us, really, and even Mr.

Everard took his wife and daughter to Saratoga to try the waters there as well as to escape the heat. Anne hadn't wanted to go, but her father wouldn't hear of her remaining in the city house by herself (even with the cook and maid there), and I was not yet in a position to whisk her away and marry her. Perhaps next year, I thought . . .

I was busy, but I did manage to get down to Rockaway for several weekends, and on one of those occasions Jennings went along with me. He said Ellen had written inviting him and suggesting that we travel down together. I was by that time pretty sure that he and Ellen were more than just good friends, and wondered what T. F. thought about the possibility of someone filling the place his son had occupied. There was, however, no sign of any disapproval on the older man's part; he was extremely fond of Ellen, may even have loved her himself, but then who didn't love my sister? Even Robert, with his stiff, reserved manner, would unbend in her presence, and young Paul spent as much time as he could with her and the children in Washington Square.

"You're the one who holds them together, Ellen, my dear," I heard T. F. say one evening when we were sitting on the veranda after dinner. "And look how happy they are."

"Well, they wouldn't be as happy in the hot city," she said with a laugh, "and who provided this lovely escape for them? Now, I ask you!"

"Nonsense!" he exclaimed, waving her gratitude away impatiently. "Aren't you all the family I have? I just wish young Paul could—"

"All he can manage is an occasional day," she said quickly, "and that's too bad. Papa—"

"He's expecting to come next Saturday," I interrupted. "I think he's been lonely since you left and he can no longer drop in at Washington Square. He comes to see me at the office once in a while instead. But I'm only second choice, Ellen; it's you he wants."

"It's a long trip down here just for the day," she murmured, "down and back by horse and buggy. What will he tell Papa?"

"Oh, probably that Mr. Downing has given him extra work that will take him all day and into the evening."

Paul was in high spirits when he appeared the following week, frolicking with the boys on the beach, teasing little Fanny until she squealed with delight, and amusing the rest of us with wicked imitations of clients who knew exactly what kind of houses they wanted the architects to design for them but found it impossible to describe them. It was one of the memorable days of that summer; there was even a letter from Annetta in Paris, which Ellen read to us while the children were having their early supper.

"Mama will be glad to hear Annetta's happy," Paul said when Ellen folded the letter back into its envelope.

"Doesn't Annetta write to her?" Robert asked.

"We don't know," Paul replied. "She may, but Papa watches for the post from his chair by the window, and then takes it in. We never see it, but I have noticed some envelopes in the trash with foreign stamps on them. German, I think."

"Probably from Cousin Hans," I said. "Remember him, Robert?"

"Who is Cousin Hans?" Paul looked perplexed.

"The son of Papa's uncle, therefore a cousin of Papa's, or so we were told," I answered. "He came to visit once, but you were too young to remember it."

"You said you never saw the mail," T. F. said in a puzzled tone. "Why, there might be a letter for you! Your father has no right—he is doing something unpardonable, even illegal—"

"He wouldn't care, T. F.," Paul said with a shrug of his shoulders. "He cares for nothing when he is angry."

"How do you stand it, Paul?" Bettina asked in her soft voice. "I can't even stand the thought of living in such a household."

"I always have room for you, Paul," Ellen said quietly. "That is, if you—"

"That would be wonderful, Ellen, but you see, I can't. To answer your question," Paul said, turning to Bettina, "I stand it for just one reason: I'd be left without a penny if I didn't. I'm not sure it's the honorable thing to do, to stay with my parents until they die so that I'll inherit what should rightfully be divided amongst the five of us. But I did swear a solemn oath to Papa that I would not leave them. He made me swear it with one hand on the Ship's Clock—that thing has some kind of religious significance for him.

"I've thought a lot about this, and I know what I'll do. If it all does come to me—and of course Papa may change his mind—I'll pass on one fifth to each of you—"

"We don't need it Paul," Ellen broke in.

"Nor do I," Robert said slowly.

"Keep it, Paul," I said. "Annetta's well off, and I am on the way up. You'll need it to set yourself up as an architect."

"Well, we'll see," Paul said. "I just wish Papa hadn't made me take that oath."

"That wasn't right," T. F. murmured in such a low voice that I think I was the only one to hear him. Then he continued, looking directly at Paul: "Of course if you've given your word to your father you must keep it, unless he agrees to release you from your promise. Would you consider asking him to do that?"

"He'd never do it, T. F. He'd more than likely berate me for daring to propose such a thing. Besides, there's Mama to consider: She needs someone there, and there's no one else except the cook. And she's no help; she's so terrified of Papa that she won't come out of the kitchen. I'm surprised she hasn't left. Mama has to put the food on the table herself.

"Look," he said, standing up and smiling at us, "don't worry about me. I'll get along. Why, a few years from now I'll be designing houses for all of you."

126

"He's a brave lad," T. F. said after we had seen Paul off in the buggy with a hamper of food on the seat beside him, "but I imagine he'll earn every cent of his inheritance."

"Yes, he will," Robert agreed, "and I certainly don't begrudge him one penny of it, but he'll get the Ship's Clock as well, and that, Papa always said, went to the oldest son. To me, that is, and then eventually to my young fellow."

"Paul will probably give it to you, Robert," Ellen said, getting up from her rocking chair. "After all, it is only an amusing toy, even if Papa seems to venerate it. Jay, will you see if the boys have cleaned up while I look after Fanny? It's almost time for dinner."

Ellen evidently did not like the turn the conversation had taken, and effectively prevented it from continuing in the same vein.

Ellen	Jay knows, I thought, when he and Robert had left to go back to the city the day after Paul's visit. Something in the manner in which he looked at me, something speculative and at the same time tolerant, convinced me that he was aware of my affair with Dan Jennings, and that he did not disapprove. Possibly because he was a doctor, as well as being my brother, he understood my need for male companionship—and physical satisfaction. And Dan provided both—not the wonderful, eager young love that had lighted the years

with Ian, but a deeper, more mature passion that glowed with a steady flame.

Whenever Dan came to me, or on the rare occasions when I went to him, from the moment he took me in his arms I relinquished myself completely to the pleasure our bodies gave each other. And afterward, when it was over and I lay with my head on his shoulder, we talked, not like young lovers, but more like husband and wife.

He would have married me in a minute, and I would gladly have agreed, had it not been for my oldest son. Philip, as I have already said, was the child who had been most deeply affected by Ian's death, and I was afraid he would turn against me if I put another man in his father's place. I saw him eyeing Dan suspiciously even before the affair began, and one day after a small tea party had dispersed he asked me why Dr. Jennings always had to sit next to me. Philip was not rude, but I had never heard him speak to Dan except in response to a direct question, in which case the answer would be brief, at times monosyllabic.

Philip's attitude may not have added perceptibly to the difficulty of conducting a clandestine affair satisfactorily, but it didn't make it any easier for us to see each other. I never went to Dan's house at night; it was too difficult to manufacture an excuse for going out alone in the dark, and of course during the day my lover was occupied with his patients. There was one lovely afternoon, though; I was shopping on Bleecker Street and suddenly felt his hand on my arm. We looked at each other for a moment, and then he guided me to the small brick house on Park Row where he had lived by himself since the death of his wife.

Did T. F. know? I wondered about that one evening shortly after our return from Rockaway. And how would he feel if he did know? Like Philip, or like Jay? Like my brother, I hoped, but how could I be sure?

The good man couldn't do enough for us, and I wouldn't want to hurt him for the world. It was typical of him to propose special outings for the children, and just before school opened that year he took Philip on a week's trip to the nation's capital, traveling by boat to Baltimore and the rest of the way by coach on the recently opened spur of the Baltimore and Ohio railroad.

"It will broaden his sights, my dear," T. F. said when he announced his plan, "and it will give me pleasure. I used to take Ian on similar outings in Australia when he was Philip's age."

Philip went off in a highly excited state, armed with a notebook in which to keep a record of the trip. I was happy for him, but at the same time I felt slightly guilty; I was secretly rejoicing that for seven days I would not have to worry about his becoming aware of Dan's nocturnal visits. What a practiced deceiver I am now, I thought gloomily—but just then I heard Dan's key in the door and flew out into the hall to welcome him.

We didn't always stay indoors and make love for the entire evening; on Friday of that week Dan took me to Castle Garden to hear Miss Jenny Lind sing. Phineas T. Barnum, it was said, paid the Swedish Nightingale one hundred and fifty thousand dollars to give a series of concerts in New York, and judging from the crowds that filled the five thousand seats in the Garden that night, his investment paid off handsomely.

"That music makes it necessary for me to make love to you for the rest of the night," Dan murmured as he sat with his arm around me in the carriage on the way home. I turned to answer him, but his lips were on mine before I could speak, and in a few moments we were approaching Washington Square. To my surprise the door was opened before we reached it, and Jay, looking agitated, hurried us inside.

"It's Papa, Ellen," he said as soon as we were in the parlor. "He's gone berserk. He was found in T. F.'s rooms at the Clarendon, emptying out the desk, throwing papers all over the place, smashing china and pottery—"

"Where is he now?" Dan asked.

"In jail, in the Tombs. Some of the other residents heard the commotion and called the manager, who notified the police. They caught me just as I was returning to the office—I'd been called out. When does T. F. get back?"

"Not until Monday," I answered. "What *are* we to do, Jay? Papa had no right—"

"Of course he had no right, Ellen. But he's crazy! Oh, God, I should have seen it coming! I don't know what will happen next, but I know this: If he's let out of jail we'll have to put him—"

"Oh, not the asylum, Jay! Not that! Oh, poor Mama."

"Then you'll have to have someone to watch him," Dan said gently. "A guard, or a keeper of some sort."

"Paul must have said something about T. F. taking Philip to Washington," I said after a few silent moments. "I can't think how else he would have known he'd be away. But why did he go there at all? What was he looking for?"

"A letter, a document of some sort, maybe," Jay said. "We may never know, but we do know that Papa took a dislike to T. F. the first time he saw him. Something happened that day that changed Papa's whole life, and it had to do with T. F."

"Could something have happened before that, something that your father was able to put out of his mind until T. F. showed up?" Dan asked. "Would your mother know anything about it?"

"I doubt it," I said. "He's been so close-mouthed . . ."

"We'll need a lawyer," Jay said, making a note on what looked like a prescription pad. "How about Ian's friend John Jay? And we'll have to let Robert know—tomorrow will be time enough for that. Maybe he can get Papa to talk to him. Papa's not as mad at him as he is at you and me. And Ellen, you'd better go around to see Mama in the morning."

Jay told me later that he went from my house down to the Tombs, where he was allowed to see Papa for fifteen minutes. "He didn't seem to know me, Ellen. He was babbling about papers with his name on them, but it was impossible to make any sense out of what he was saying. I stayed as long as the guard would let me, but I can't say I accomplished anything. If only—oh, I just don't know—what are we to do?"

★ ★ ★

131

In the end we were not called upon to make arrangements for my father's care. He died sometime during the night after Jay left him. Of a stroke, we heard. In a way, his death was a relief to us, but that is not to say that no one mourned his passing. My brothers kept their own counsel, and the very fact that they refrained from any criticism or condemnation of Papa made me wonder if they, like me, regretted that they hadn't made more of an effort to understand him. My mother, though stunned at the suddenness of his death, kept a tight rein on her emotions. All she said, as the carriage bore us to the funeral ceremony, was that from now on she would think of Papa only as he had been when they were both young.

"Now I'll never know what caused the antipathy he felt for me and for Ian," T. F. said to me after we had seen the coffin lowered into the grave in St. Paul's churchyard. "Had I been able to fathom that riddle I would have done everything in my power to right any wrong."

"He was the one to wrong you, T. F.," I said. "Look at the damage he did to your rooms and—"

"My dear Ellen, he was not responsible. A deranged mind— and what did he actually do? Threw some papers around, broke a few pieces of china, nothing of great value. Don't concern yourself with that. The basic question is twofold: First, what did he hold against me all these years, and second, what did he think I had in my possession that involved him in some way? Whatever the answers are, he has taken them to the grave with him. Come, I see your mother waiting in the carriage. Perhaps she can throw some light on the subject."

But my mother remained silent. If she had any knowledge of the affair that had puzzled us for so long, she volunteered nothing. The only comment I heard her make concerning Papa's death was, "Perhaps it was time." She knew nothing about any papers that might have been relevant to the past, and when Robert went through the desk in Papa's bedroom he found only a checkbook, a few receipted tradesmen's bills, and the will. Everything had been left to Mama and was to go to Paul on her death, provided he remained living with her. She told Paul he could move out any time he liked, that she would leave the money to him anyway, but he just shook his head.

The two of them continued to live in the Henry Street house, comfortably, according to Paul. "Mama no longer has to bring the food to the table," he said with a smile. "Sophie has finally come out of her hiding place."

When Jay commented on how contented Mama seemed, Robert nodded and said that in his opinion it was because for the first time in years she was able to do as she pleased. He was right, too; even before the prescribed year of mourning was out she was giving small dinner parties (mostly family affairs), and entertaining members of a sewing circle at tea, things she wouldn't have dared do while Papa was alive.

And Paul was thriving. In 1853 Calvert Vaux, a young architect who had worked in Downing's office for a while, collaborated with Frederick Law Olmsted, and together they won a national competition for the best design for a city park. Vaux enlisted Paul's help on the project, and for the next few years my younger brother was engrossed in the development of Central Park. As the work progressed Paul's name became better known, and in a relatively short time he was a well-established architect with his own set of offices. He never did design a house for me, but sometime in the late 1850s Robert, who could well afford it, had him draw up plans for an elegant town house on Fifth Avenue to accommodate himself, Bettina, and their son, Alex. The mantelpiece in the large drawing room was especially designed to show the Ship's Clock to advantage. Paul had given it to Robert for Christmas the year Papa died.

Jay, to Mama's delight, married Anne Everard, who presented him with three children in rapid succession. I wondered briefly if my mother would give her the same advice she had once given me . . .

Dan and I continued to snatch precious, all-too-infrequent hours together, every moment of which I cherished, but it wasn't enough for either of us. I wanted to feel him next to me in bed when I stirred during the night, and to see his head on the pillow when I awoke. But when he suggested that I go away with him for a weekend, I couldn't bring myself to do it.

"Then we must get married, darling," he said. "I won't give you up, and we shouldn't have to go on like this."

He'd asked me several times to have a talk with Philip, explaining to him that a second marriage on my part would in no way indicate that I was unfaithful to his father's memory, that on the other hand, I would be doing what Ian would have wished: insuring that my children live a normal family life. I was tempted—oh, how I longed to have done with the secretiveness, the deceit, and the worry our meetings necessitated—but I was still too fearful of losing the affection of my oldest child to act on my lover's advice. I could see all too clearly, though, that we couldn't continue in the same way much longer.

We'd been lucky so far, Dan pointed out, but as the children grew older it would be increasingly difficult to hide our relationship from them. And hadn't I noticed that we were able to be alone less and less frequently as time went on? I admitted that what he said was true, and said that I didn't like it any more than he did, but still I hesitated. Then, in the fall of that year Dan took matters into his own hands.

On a rainy Saturday morning in late October I was sitting by the fire with a copy of the city's newest newspaper, *The New York Times,* when the maid announced Dr. Jennings. I was surprised that he would call so early in the day, and a bit startled when I saw how serious, almost grim, he looked.

Without any preliminaries or explanation he asked me if all the children were at home, and if so, would I send for them.

Once they were assembled in the parlor he lined them up (Fanny asked if they were going to play London Bridge Is Falling Down), and standing a short distance away, looked at each one in turn before he spoke.

"I have an important announcement to make," he said in a low but firm voice. "I intend to marry your mother. Does anyone have any objection to that?"

My eyes flew to Philip's face, and I felt my heart skip a beat. All five of them stared at Dan in silence, and then to my great relief and astonishment Philip smiled and said he thought it would be a good idea if I had someone to take care of me when he went off to college. He was only fifteen then but had evidently been considering himself the man of the house.

"What about the rest of you?" Dan asked. "Do you agree with Philip?"

They all nodded seriously, and John said he thought John Jennings sounded like a better name than John Ferguson. Dan explained that for the time being they would all keep the Ferguson name, but later on, when they were of age, they could make any change they liked.

"And on the subject of names," he went on, "I suggest that you continue to call me Doctor Dan. I am not your father, and I do not want to be called 'Stepfather.' Are you agreeable to that?"

They all nodded again, and then Dan shook hands with each one, bending low to take Fanny's little palm in his, after which he said he would like to speak to me privately. I sent them down to the kitchen for cocoa and oatmeal cookies, a Saturday morning ritual, and when we heard them clattering down the stairs Dan turned to me, smiling broadly.

"I should have done that long ago," he said ruefully. "Why didn't I?"

"Because you were as concerned about Philip's reaction as I was," I replied. "And it might not have worked out then, my dear. But by now, the memory of Ian's death has faded, and

Philip's found out that he likes you. The other boys have always accepted you, and of course Fanny adores you."

"And you?" he asked, taking me in his arms and holding me close to him.

We were married quietly the following week, and Dan moved into my house on Washington Square.

No one seemed too surprised at our marriage. T. F., about whose reaction I'd had some concern, smiled happily and said he'd seen it coming; Mama said how nice it was now that she'd have more opportunities to speak German to Dan; Robert said he was glad I'd found a man who wasn't a fortune hunter; Paul wanted to know if he should start on plans for a house for us; and Jay rightfully took the credit for bringing us together.

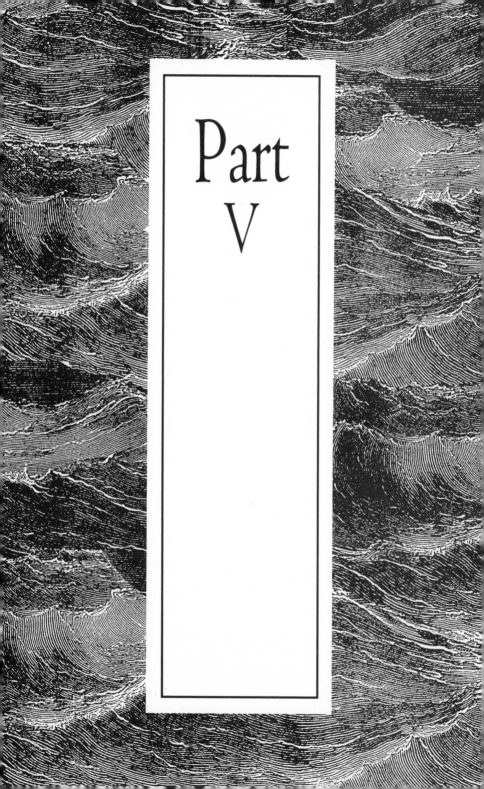

Part
V

New
York,
1860

Ellen

On the morning of Saturday, February 25, 1860, I coaxed, cajoled, pleaded, and finally persuaded the members of my immediate family to accompany me to the photographic studio of Mr. Mathew Brady at 643 Broadway to sit for a group portrait. Only with difficulty did I manage to override the various objections and excuses presented to me at the breakfast table: hair that required trimming (Rodney), a visit to the law library (John), suspicion of an incipient sore throat (Will), and the likelihood of being late for an important luncheon engagement (Philip). Only Fanny, who had a new dress for the occasion, showed any enthusiasm at the prospect of posing for the camera. Dan said nothing at all but sat through the meal with an air of quiet amusement.

I am glad I persisted: The photographic study that Mr. Brady produced is the only record I have of what we were like in 1860, before tragedy struck. Twenty-three-year-old Philip, who, to T. F.'s delight, was working for an import-export house, looks remarkably like Ian in the picture. He has the same tall, slender frame, the same alert gray eyes, and Ian's thick dark brown hair. Next to him stands Roddy, big and burly at twenty-one, grinning happily at the camera. Never a student, my second son left school at the age of fifteen to work for a construction company, where he was making slow but steady advances. My serious Johnny, who was reading law at Ian's old firm of Willebrandt and Pyne, is wedged between big Roddy and lanky Will, who at sixteen was already determined to become a doctor and was never happier than when Dan or Jay permitted him to make calls with them.

In the picture, Dan and I are seated in front of the row of boys, and a smiling Fanny, resplendent in her crinolines, stands beside Dan, one hand resting lightly on his shoulder. Dan's handsome head is turned slightly toward me, and although the twinkle in his eyes is not visible I am sure it is there, since he told me later he could scarcely keep from laughing at the triumphant (his word) expression on my face. I suppose it was in a way a triumph for me to persuade them all to give up a Saturday morning for me, but then . . .

The boys' spirits rose when Mr. Brady informed us that a Republican named Lincoln was expected to sit for his portrait the following Monday.

"Lincoln, did you say? You mean the man who lost to Stephen A. Douglas?" Johnny asked excitedly. "He's—"

"He's going to speak at the Cooper Union on Monday night," Philip broke in, "and I'm going to be there. We should all go!"

"Even me? Please, Ma!" Fanny begged.

"Yes! You must let Fan come, Ma! He's a man who will make history!"

"And he's not apt to give her nightmares like the ones she had after you took her to see the freaks at Barnum's, Roddy," Dan said, patting the top of Fanny's curly head. "I agree that we should all go, Ellen," he added when he saw me hesitating.

★ ★ ★

Even though it was snowing heavily that Monday night, we did all go to hear Mr. Lincoln, and he did make history with his speech. When he stood up on the stage after Mr. William Cullen Bryant's introduction he appeared ill at ease, and at first his voice betrayed his nervousness. After a few minutes, however, he gained confidence, his voice deepened, and for an hour and a half he held the audience of some fifteen hundred people spellbound. His main topic was the threat of the spread of slavery to the free states, and speaking with restrained eloquence, he urged us to give the problem calm consideration, keeping in mind that "right makes might."

Never have I heard anything like the wild cheering and thunderous applause that resounded through the Great Hall of the Cooper Union when the tall man in the ill-fitting black suit bowed and resumed his seat on the stage. I was as moved as anyone by Lincoln's impassioned plea. Now, however, I look back on that evening with mixed emotions. Dan thinks my three older boys would have enlisted in the Union Army whether they'd heard the speech or not, but I cannot help wondering if things might have been different had I not persuaded them to accompany me to Mathew Brady's studio.

A little over a year later, on April 15, 1861, Lincoln asked for seventy-five thousand volunteers for three months' service in the army. Philip, Roddy, and John signed up at once. I try not to dwell on the horrors and sorrows of the next five years, but I know I will never be able to forget them. John was killed at Shiloh in the spring of 1862, and Philip bled to death at Fredericksburg in December of that year. Dan, who was working in the field hospital there, was with him at the end.

And Will, poor innocent, crippled Will, was accosted on the street one July day in 1863 by a group of enraged Irishmen who were protesting the draft. They accused him of paying three hundred dollars for a substitute, and turned ugly when he denied having done so.

"Three hundred dollars is me pay for a year's work," one of the men shouted at him, "and look at yer foine clothes and boots—git him, b'hoys!"

It could have been worse; Will was knocked to the ground, but before he was beaten the group was distracted by the arrival of an angry mob of men and women armed with muskets, clubs, and even cobblestones. He barely managed to drag himself to safety behind a couple of empty beer barrels before the frenzied crowd surged past on their way to the enrollment office on Third Avenue, shouting "down with the draft" as they went, thus setting off one of the worst riots in New York's history.

For the next four days no right-thinking citizen ventured out into the streets. A pall of smoke from the fires set by the rioters hung over the city, and no one could tell when his house might be broken into. Stores were looted: Brooks Brothers, at Catherine and Cherry streets, known for the fine quality of its men's clothing, was invaded by an inflamed mob, some of whose members emerged wearing expensive overcoats on top of their rags, and high silk hats on their heads. Women were just as bad, grabbing up articles of clothing indiscriminately to take home to their menfolk, and trampling on what they could not carry. Outside, horse cars were upended, and carriages and wagons were damaged beyond repair.

The worst of the human suffering was among the Negro population; the maddened, liquor-crazed mobs blamed the war, and therefore the draft, on the Negros, and in their frenzy beat, killed, or tortured any Negro they encountered. The colored orphanage on Fifth Avenue and Forty-fourth Street, housing two hundred children, was burned to the ground, but fortunately all but one of the orphans escaped through a rear door.

After four days of bloody fighting in the streets, on the squares, in public buildings, and in private residences, three regiments, our own Seventh among them, were recalled from the war's front to disperse the mob. The soldiers acted quickly and efficiently, and order was restored to the city in a remarkably short time, a blessed relief to all of us.

It was not, however, a time for rejoicing. During the calm that followed the riots, the tragic consequences of the war were all too evident in the lists of dead and wounded that appeared daily in the newspapers. Our personal lives were no less gloomy than the national scene: Two of my sons were gone forever, and Jay, who had followed Dan into field hospital work, was sent home with a badly wounded left arm. The entire world seemed dark to me, with a deeper darkness approaching, threatening to envelop us all.

T. F., who moved in with us when the rioting began, was a steadying influence on our distraught household. His very presence seemed to have a calming effect on Fanny, Will, and myself, as well as on Mama, who spent more and more time with us as the days dragged by. She'd arrive sometime during the afternoon and stay until Paul came for her on his way home from work. T. F. spent more time with her than I did, occasionally taking her out for what he called an "airing" in a hired carriage, but generally simply keeping her company in the parlor while I nursed my grief alone in my bedroom.

I wish now I'd been more considerate, less self-centered; I didn't even notice that Mama wasn't looking well until T. F. called it to my attention one evening.

"She's rather pale, Ellen," he said thoughtfully, "and seems to tire easily. Also, she's so quiet—speaks so little—that I have the impression there is something on her mind, something that worries her. Of course, I do not feel I can ask any prying questions."

"Oh, don't fuss over me, Ellen," Mama said crossly when I spoke to her the following day. "Of course I tire easily; it is part of growing old. You will notice the same thing when you are my age. Now go about your business. T. F. will keep me company while I finish this sweater for Will."

I left the two of them sitting by the fire and went upstairs, thinking that perhaps Jay ought to have a look at her, but I hated to bother him while his arm was so painful. Whether he could have done any good or not I shall never know, for it was only a few days later that my mother collapsed while dining with Robert and Bettina.

Robert   During the days that my mother hovered between life and death in the large front bedroom on the third floor of my house, I spent more hours alone with her than I had in all the years of my life. Ellen, Paul, and Jay came for short visits each day, but the nurse said that only when I was at the bedside, holding her hand, did my mother seem at peace. Since she had never given any indication of having a favorite among her children, I was at first at a loss to explain her preference for my company over that of the others. In the end, however, I understood that affection had nothing to do with the matter.

For three or four days she lay quietly, sleeping lightly, speaking only when necessary, but on the fifth evening she surprised me by asking the nurse to leave us. After the door closed, she turned a calm thoughtful gaze on me, and said it was time I knew certain things.

"Ever since Papa died," she began, "no, even before that,

I have debated with myself which is the right thing for me to do: to keep silent, or to tell what I know, the secret he kept for all these years. But to whom should I speak, I asked myself. And I decided to tell you, Robert, since you are the oldest of my children. And I trust you. You will know what to do.

"I hope you will neither disbelieve me nor think ill of me for keeping silent for so long, for what I have to tell you is bound to surprise and shock you. I thought of confiding in Ellen, but then what with Philip and John dying and her worry about Doctor Dan and Rodney, I was reluctant to burden her further."

"I understand, Mama," I said when she stopped speaking and closed her eyes for a moment, "but what—"

"And I thought of Jay," she went on so softly that I could hardly hear her. "But he is not yet strong. His poor arm . . . And Paul, I did not even consider Paul. So it had to be you, and I will tell you but once. Your father, Robert, was not who you were brought up to believe he was—"

"You mean he was not my father?" I was aghast.

"Oh, yes, he was the father of all of you, but there was this: There was a curse put upon him, and upon all his sons. When he stole the Ship's Clock—you didn't know about that—and he did other bad things—his own father put the curse on him and on the clock, and it continues on to you and Jay and Paul, no matter what Papa's name was, and his name was not John Fergus—ah—ah—aie . . ."

She gasped, as one in extreme pain, at the same time gripping my hand with all her strength. I shouted for the nurse, who came running, and after one look at her patient administered a sedative. I sat watching until the drug took effect and my mother's fingers relaxed in my hand.

"She won't wake up for three or four hours now, Mr. Ferguson," the nurse said. "Shall I send for you when she does?"

146

"By all means. I want to be with her when she awakens."

The nurse nodded, but from the expression on her face I thought she might only be humoring me, as one does a child, and that she really did not have much hope that my mother would regain consciousness.

She did, though. Just as the clock in the hall struck midnight she opened her eyes and tried to speak. Her lips moved, and at first no sound came, but as I leaned close to her I thought I heard her say: "The curse—on Philip—his sons—his father—"

I pressed her hand gently to encourage her to go on, but those few whispered words were her last.

During the weeks that followed my mother's death I puzzled constantly over the meaning of her unfinished message, and pondered over questions to which I could find no answer:

1. If John Ferguson was my father, why was he not the man I thought he was?
2. Philip? Ellen's son? What had he to do with my father?
3. The curse—a curse. On Philip? Why?
4. Whose father was she talking about at the last?
5. Shall I confer with the others or not?

As my mother had said, it would be unkind to trouble Ellen, to add anything unpleasant to the burdens she already carried. She'd been right about Jay, too; while he tried to minimize the extent of his injury, it was obvious to me that he was deeply concerned about regaining the full use of his arm and hand. That left my youngest brother.

Neither Paul nor I took part in the war between the North and the South. He had a legitimate excuse for not signing up, a pronounced murmur of the heart, but I consider my alibi to have been spurious. I think I would have enlisted if it hadn't been for Bettina, who became almost hysterical every time the subject came up.

"Do you want to leave Alex and me to fend for ourselves?" she argued one night shortly after the riots had been subdued. "Have you no concern for our welfare? What will become of us if you get yourself killed?" And so on, and so on. She also pointed out that I was fifty years of age in 1863, and would not be able to tolerate the hardships of battle in the manner of a twenty-year-old. She had a point there, I suppose, but still . . .

In the end I gave in to her, and salved my conscience by contributing heavily to some of the many charitable organizations that had been formed to aid the widows and children of soldiers, but I am not proud of myself.

Paul, on the other hand, took his rejection philosophically.

"Perhaps it's for the best," he said. "Now I know I have a wonky heart. The army doctor warned me not to overexert, to take care of myself. Plenty of sleep and fresh air, he said, and be careful what I eat. Things I've never paid any attention to."

Immediately after seeing the doctor he came to see me at my office, the large corner one now that I was president of the bank. In spite of his cheerful, almost carefree manner of speaking, signs of worry were apparent in his eyes and furrowed brow. My gay, lighthearted brother was, for the first time in his life, giving thought to his own mortality. But not for long.

From that time on, instead of following the doctor's advice, instead of cutting back on his working hours and taking care of himself, Paul accepted more and more commissions, hired more staff, and drove himself as hard as he drove his employees. He brushed off any suggestions that he slow down, claiming that he throve on a program of hard work during the day and hard play at night.

After Mama's death the house on Henry Street became a gathering place for his cronies, all young men about his age,

and all either architects, actors (Paul had always been ena-
moured of the theater), or artists. Some nights they'd all go to
Pfaff's Tavern, down on Broadway near Bleecker Street, and
join a group he called the Bohemians. When I asked him what
the attraction there was he answered somewhat vaguely.

"Oh, we sit around in the alcove Pfaff reserves for us,
and talk—good talk—interesting fellows, those writers.
Edgar Allen Poe was one of the group once." That worried
me; I'd heard a good deal about what a dissolute character
Mr. Poe was.

Although I had reason to believe that liquor flowed freely
on those occasions, I had no proof that Paul was drinking more
than was good for him—but I wondered. I mentioned my
concern to Jay when he came to the bank to see about investing a fairly considerable sum Anne had recently inherited.

"You're probably right, Rob," he said after a moment's
thought. "It sometimes goes this way: A person learns that his
heart or liver is not functioning properly (this arm of mine is
a different case entirely) and makes up his mind that death
could strike at any moment. As a consequence, he resolves to
throw discretion to the winds and fill whatever time remains
to him with whatever experiences he most enjoys. *Carpe diem!*
Of course there are those who react reasonably, who follow
the physician's advice, and lead quiet, if dull lives. Obviously
Paul has elected the first option."

"What if he should marry? Wouldn't it be good for him to
settle down with a wife and family?"

"I doubt that Paul will ever marry," Jay answered as he
stood up to leave. "He told me he didn't think it right to start
a family when he had no idea how long his heart would last.
He has a point there, I suppose, and actually he's quite happy
as things are. Naturally I wish he'd listen to the doctors, but
I'm afraid he'll never slow down. He's almost as stubborn as
Papa was.

"Look, I must be on my way, Rob. I've a patient to see at

St. Luke's before I go home. Thanks for the financial advice. Anne and I depend on you in these matters."

No, I thought as the door closed on Jay, I won't tell anyone about Mama's last words, at least for the present. There's always the possibility that her mind was not clear, that she was imagining things. She was, after all, within a few minutes of death when she tried to reveal whatever dark secret she thought she knew. And whatever it was, she'd left it too late.

"Damnation," I said under my breath, and turned to the papers on my desk, annoyed that I had spent so much time on family matters when there were markets to watch and money to be made.

Ellen

When the war ended and Roddy and Dan, looking thin and weary, came home to us, I made a concentrated effort to put sorrow aside and dispel the gloom that for so many long months had hung over the household. I had fallen into the habit of brooding over the deaths—Ian's, Papa's Mama's, and most of all, those of Philip and Johnny. Hours on end I'd spend alone in my room, staring idly into the fire, making no effort to respond to well-meant suggestions that I rouse myself and go about a bit. I even snapped impatiently at Will and Fanny when they sought to comfort me, and sent them away peremptorily.

Dan's letter saying he was on his way home accomplished what my children could not do: It jolted me out of my self-indulgence. After a long look in my glass (I had neglected my appearance for months) I surprised the life out of Fanny and T. F. by ordering a carriage and making the rounds of the hair-dresser, the shoe store, the dressmaker, and the milliner, a woman's way of making the world look brighter, I suppose.

Fanny was a great help. I'd been so wrapped up in myself that I hadn't realized how deeply in love she was with young Wesley Bannister, a friend of Will's who worked in Brentano's Book Store on lower Fifth Avenue. Suddenly I realized that she was simply radiating the happiness of first love, young love, such as I had experienced with Ian. It'd been wonderful with Dan, but different . . .

When winter set in Fanny persuaded me to resume the Sunday supper "gathering of the clan," as she called it, which would now include Wesley, of course. She also enlisted my help in assembling her trousseau and in planning the wedding, which was to take place on April 15, 1866, her eighteenth birthday. Then there was Dan's old house on Park Row to be refurbished. His tenants had moved away when the father of the family failed to return from the war, and it had stood empty for some six months or so.

Not only did my thoughtful husband offer it to Fan and Wesley at a ridiculously low rental, but he also undertook to have it cleaned, painted, and papered if they would choose the colors and patterns.

"You and your Ma had better do that, Fan," Wesley said when he was asked to choose between two shades of green for the walls of the little parlor. "I'd get it wrong. But let me see to the bookshelves in the study."

Scarcely a day passed that winter that we weren't poring over samples of paint, or matching swatches of material for curtains, or hurrying down to the Ladies' Mile to choose carpets at W. and J. Sloane's, or linens at Lord and Taylor's Dry Goods store.

Fan's happiness and high spirits carried over to the rest of us, and that, along with Dan's deep, unaltered love, enabled me to put the past in proper perspective. Left to myself I might never have emerged from the depths to which I had sunk.

★ ★ ★

After the wedding, Dan and I had more time alone than we'd ever had before. Roddy and Will, the only two we had left at home, were so busy with their own affairs that we saw little of them. Roddy's construction firm, Belknap and Company, welcomed him back to a thriving business. New buildings were going up constantly as Manhattan residents moved farther and farther uptown, leaving lower New York to commercial and financial enterprises, and as a result Roddy was on constant call. Any free evenings he had were given over to courting Adela Belknap, whom I had yet to meet. I could only hope that my son was truly in love, and that he did not look upon marriage with his employer's daughter merely as a means of furthering his career. It was hard to tell with Roddy.

Will practically lived at St. Luke's Hospital, where he was a resident physician, and could seldom take time off from his duties. According to Jay he was, not unexpectedly, devoting as much time as he could spare from his patients to searching for means of correcting malformations of the foot.

"When he sees a person with a club foot, Ellen, especially if it's a child, he can't do enough. He's so good with them, so compassionate and encouraging that they almost fall down and worship him." Jay paused for a moment, smiling and shaking his head in admiration for his nephew. "He told me once that if he can convince a youngster that his deformed foot needn't either ruin or control his life, he feels almost as if he has effected a cure. Will's going to be a great doctor."

I had never doubted that Will would make a success of his professional life, and said as much, but I did not voice my fears about his personal happiness. I could only hope that someday he would find a girl to whom his poor foot made no difference. Like the rest of us, however, he seemed happy enough during the four or five years following the war, years that Dan labeled "our own period of reconstruction."

Dan himself made a change. Instead of resuming his practice

he elected to teach medicine at Columbia College, a choice that enabled him to count on regular hours, and far more free time than he'd had before the war. Time to spend with me, he said. He made a point of taking me to the theater, and out to dine at a posh restaurant at least once a week. He particularly enjoyed going to the St. Nicholas Hotel, where the soft-shell crabs à l'Anglaise and roast partridge with celery sauce were specialties, or to the Fifth Avenue Hotel for their baked oysters. We went only once to the Hoffman House to try their famous duck with Canton ginger, but found the smell of their equally famous Hoffman House cigars (smoked by the numerous politicians who gathered there) an unpleasant accompaniment to the meal.

"I'll give you another reason for not patronizing the Hoffman House," Jay said when I told him of our experience. "Did you know that when single gentlemen stay there they are apt to find an engraved invitation to visit 'The Seven Sisters' on their breakfast trays?"

"You mean the musical play?"

"No, not at all, my dear sister," he answered with a laugh. "I mean the high-class brothel on Twenty-seventh Street that boasts of having seven parlors, each one containing a lovely lady in evening dress."

So much for the Hoffman House.

In the spring of 1869 Dan suggested that we take the honeymoon we never had and spend the summer abroad.

"I have no classes in July and August, love, so we could have a good eight weeks there, traveling around wherever you like. We could see Annetta; didn't you say she'd been urging you to visit her? And wouldn't you like that?"

I hated to disappoint him, but I had promised to be on hand for the birth of Fanny's second child, due late in July. "She needs me, Dan," I said. "You know how sick she's been all through this pregnancy. I couldn't leave her."

"Of course not, darling. Next summer will do just as well. But we'd better not put it off too long; we're not far from three score, you know."

But we did not go abroad the following summer, and for a while it looked as if we never would. The lovely respite we'd had from riots, battles, illness and deaths, came to an abrupt end on September 24, 1869, a day still referred to as Black Friday.

James	My last patient that Friday, a wealthy old woman who lived on Lafayette Street in one of the mansions of Colonnade Row, was not a pleasant person. She berated me and the entire medical profession for not being able to cure her varicose veins, carrying on for a good ten minutes in a voice both sharp and querulous. Why is it, I wondered as I emerged from her marble hallway into the September sunlight, that the poor are so much more apt to be reasonable about illness than the rich? Then I reminded myself to

beware of generalizations . . .

It had been a long day, and I was looking forward to a quiet evening with Anne, but as I approached the house we had bought with her inheritance (instead of investing in the stock market) just two doors down from Ellen and Dan, I saw young Alex running toward me.

"Mother sent me," he gasped. "Father's been taken ill! I've a cab waiting—Hurry, Uncle Jay!"

***

Ten minutes later I was kneeling on the carpet beside the sofa where Robert lay staring vacantly at the ceiling of his front parlor. An anguished Bettina was rubbing his hands and whispering endearments that fell on deaf ears, while three gentlemen, bank employees, I assumed, stood quietly to one side.

"Has he spoken at all?" I asked Bettina, who shook her head without taking her eyes from Robert's face.

It was not until he'd been carried up to his room and made as comfortable as possible in the large canopied bed that I could turn my attention to the men who had been with him. From Mr. Bertram Elgin, who identified himself as a vice president of the bank, I learned of the day's debacle on Wall Street and the widespread panic among financiers. I do not recall his exact words, but the gist of what he said is as follows:

Robert had been in the Gold Room, as the Gold Exchange at the corner of Exchange Place and Broad Street was known, when word came that the Sub Treasury would sell four million dollars' worth of gold the following day. Somehow he managed to make his way out of the pandemonium that raged after that announcement and back to the bank, where he spent the rest of the day locked in his office.

"At five o'clock we were worried," Elgin said. "The bank was closing, doors were being locked, and he would not answer to our knocking or calling out. Finally Briggs here, and Anderson, forced the door, and we found him slumped down across the desk, with papers and stock certificates all over the place. Not like Mr. Ferguson at all—he was a demon for neatness and order.

"He was conscious, sir, and did not protest when we helped him stand up and then assisted him into a cab. We managed to get him into the house and onto the sofa, where you saw him."

"Did he say anything at all to you?" I asked.

"Only mutterings and groans. I imagine he suffered heavy losses with today's slide. And I know he was hard hit a while back when the Erie Railroad went broke. Briggs, did you hear him say anything?"

"Not clearly, sir, but something he said sounded like 'gone, gone.' "

More than Robert's fortune was gone. He never fully recovered either physically or mentally from the crash of 1869. Dan Jennings agreed with me that he had suffered a slight stroke while in his office on Black Friday, and a second, more severe one just after entering his Fifth Avenue house. He was left with slurred speech, as well as a paralysis that rendered his right arm and leg useless. My major concern, and Dan concurred, was that full realization of the extent of his financial ruin would bring on a third stroke. But Robert surprised us.

"I knew it all along, Jay," he said later in his halting way. "I knew I was ruined." (I will make no attempt to reproduce his slurred speech.) I was sitting with him in his room in Ellen's house—his own had been sold at auction, along with all its expensive furnishings. My good sister turned over an entire floor to him and his family, and in addition provided a male attendant for Robert. "I've been expecting something like this ever since Mama died—"

He broke off in midsentence and closed his eyes, leaving me to wonder what he meant. When he spoke again, it was to ask me how I had weathered the crash. I told him we'd put Anne's money into the new house instead of investing in stocks and bonds, and he nodded.

"That's good," he said slowly. "At least I didn't cause you to be ruined. Those railroad shares—I put all the money I made on the Water Street property into them, and when they went down I thought I could recoup by buying gold. It went to one sixty, and I was set to sell at two hundred; then I would have been safe. But you know what happened; Jay Gould and Jim Fisk ought to be drawn and quartered for rigging the market. Damn it all! But I'm glad you're all right."

———

158

I made a point of dropping in to see him at least once a day, generally for only ten or fifteen minutes, but on occasion, if I had the time and if Robert felt like talking, the visit would be longer. One afternoon in particular stands out in my memory. Wallace, the attendant, was off that day, and Bettina, always fearful that Robert might need more assistance than she could provide, welcomed me gratefully.

"He's been asking for you all day long, Jay," she said, "and keeps saying he must tell you something. What it is I can't imagine, but I beg you to give him a chance to get it off his mind. I'll go down and visit with Ellen. Wallace wheeled him into the front room before he left. Go on, now! He probably saw you coming—he's been watching out the window."

Just like Papa, I thought—remembering what Paul had said about my father watching for the postman—and not like the old Robert.

He looked up expectantly as I entered the room, and with his good arm motioned to a chair that had been drawn up to face him.

"Has Bettina gone out?" he asked in a whisper. "I wouldn't like her to hear this."

I assured him that she had gone downstairs to see Ellen, and he leaned back in his chair, closing his eyes for a moment or two.

"I know now what Mama meant," he said finally. "She was trying to warn me that something like this would happen."

"Rob, how could she possibly foresee—"

"Oh, not this specifically," he said impatiently, pointing to his useless leg. "Just listen, Jay; give me a chance. I wasn't going to tell anyone, because at first I thought it was all nonsense, that she was imagining things, but now that I've reasoned it out, and before it's too late—oh, I know I'm failing and haven't much longer—I've decided to tell you.

"In a way it helps explain Papa's behavior. You remember how little he spoke of his early life, don't you? I used to think of him as being born full grown here in New York. Well, there's a reason for his reticence. Apparently he disobeyed his father, which means his story about his father's death when he was a year old is a lie. What man would put a curse on an infant? No, don't interrupt!

"Just before she died Mama said that Papa's father had been so angry with him—I didn't know he'd stolen the Ship's Clock, did you? Anyway, his father, according to Mama, was so enraged that he put a curse on Papa and on the clock, and any sons he might have. So Papa changed his name. Mama had a seizure before she could tell me what it was originally, but she said it was not Ferguson. Who are we, anyway?"

"Surely you don't believe all that, Robert? The vagaries of a dying woman's mind? Mama wasn't—"

"Well, just look, Jay: Papa crippled for years and years, struck down in his prime, you might say, and almost mad. Then take me, a pauper as well as a cripple. Then there's Paul, with a bad heart, drinking himself to death, and your war wound. I think Mama felt guilty that she hadn't warned us years ago, although God knows whether we would have paid any attention to her then."

"And if I were you," I said as lightly as I could, "I wouldn't pay any attention now to what she said when she was dying. Oh, you make a good case for the calamities that have befallen us to be attributed to a long-ago curse, but I simply cannot accept it. Supernatural rot."

"Believe what you like, Jay. It's off my mind—no, that's not true; it will always be on my mind. If only I had my strength and health back! I'd go to Germany and see who our forbears really were, and perhaps lay the ghost to rest. Why don't you go, Jay? Find out *who* we are? Our real name?"

I told him I'd think about it, and I did, but not too seriously. When Ellen and Dan announced that they were planning a trip to Europe that summer Rob was delighted, and made them promise to look up Cousin Hans Mesner if they did nothing else.

"Find out what he knows, Ellen, find out, find out!" Dear God, I can still hear him . . .

Ellen

On a bright June morning in 1871 Dan and I at last embarked on our trip to Europe, sailing on the *Oceanica*, the pride of the White Star Line, with strict instructions from Robert to leave no stone unturned in an effort to find the connection between Cousin Hans Mesner and Papa and Mama.

"It stands to reason, Ellen," he said just before we left, "that Cousin Hans would know Papa's family, and therefore his real name. We know that Papa lied about the Ship's Clock—about how his father gave it to him. Mama said he stole it—and God knows what else he lied about. And that business about the curse, see what you can find out about that. But the *name* is the important thing. If it isn't Ferguson—oh, I've told you what Mama said."

Indeed he had told me, a dozen times or more; he seemed to think and talk about nothing else at the time, and although *I* thought it was all probably nonsense I promised to see what I could find out. I had thought Jay was just as skeptical as I was, but just before we sailed he reminded me that Papa had never talked about his life in Germany if he could help it.

"Perhaps there is a reason why he was so close-mouthed, Ellen," he said, "but I doubt that you'll be able to unearth it after all these years. I wouldn't spend too much time trying if I were you. This is supposed to be a pleasure trip for you and Dan."

Before going on to Hamburg we spent a wonderful, unforgettable fortnight with Annetta in Paris. At the age of forty-seven my sister was still striking enough to cause heads to turn when we entered a restaurant, or sat in her box at the opera, or went with her to see the treasures of the Louvre. Her husband, Pierre, now the owner of the Du Champs gallery in the Rue de la Paix, made a special effort to entertain us, too, treating us as if we were visiting royalty. But it was Annetta's beauty and happiness that impressed me most, and I made a point of saying so the evening before we were due to leave.

"I don't know about the beauty," she said with a little smile. "I can see it fading, but the happiness has been lasting. I'll tell you one thing, Ellen dear: If I had stayed in New York under Papa's thumb one week, even one day longer than I did, I think I would have done something awful—murder, perhaps. Oh, don't look so shocked! It would not have come to that, but I had to get out, and Pierre came along at just the right time. And, as you can see, *he* is a wonderful father, not like ours."

Not a bit like ours, I thought as I watched Pierre and his two teen-aged daughters laughing over a book of caricatures he had brought home. Not one little bit like ours.

It came as no surprise to me that no one by the name of Ferguson could be located in the city of Hamburg. Neither was there a Hans Mesner. We found, however, that a firm by the name of Mesner and Sons existed, and made our way to an ancient stone building on the Hafenplatz near the banks of the Elbe. Hans Mesner was no longer alive, but his son, Gottfried, asked if he could be of help.

"You say my father visited you in New York, Mrs. Jennings?" he asked in heavily accented English. "And that you are his cousin?"

"Yes, indeed. We were told to call him Cousin Hans, so naturally when we saw the name of your firm—"

"Of course, of course, you thought you would look him up! I would have done the same thing. My father was indeed Hans Mesner, but I know nothing of any cousins in America. But come in, come in and sit down!"

He ushered us into a large office with small leaded glass windows overlooking the river, and while he was ordering coffee to be brought my attention was caught by a most remarkable porcelain stove standing in one corner.

"Ah, yes," Herr Mesner said when I commented on the beauty of the blue and white tiles. "It has been in the family for generations. Come closer to see it better. See, it tells here the story of Solomon's Judgment. It is a genuine antique, except for a few tiles here and there that had to be replaced due to an accident years ago. I have never heard exactly what happened; probably some servant became careless."

Over coffee, hot, strong, and sweet, we gathered that Gottfried Mesner could not enlighten us about the relationship between my father and mother and Hans Mesner, and that he, Gottfried, had never heard the name Ferguson.

"However," he said as he handed around a plate of pastries, "my father traveled a great deal on business in his younger days, and he may well have been in your city. Perhaps he had business with your father, and 'Cousin' was just a courtesy title."

I was afraid he'd think me mad if I said anything about trying to find out what my father's real name was, so I pretended to agree with him. He let it go at that, and the conversation became general. We chatted pleasantly for a short time, and then, after extracting a promise from us that we would dine at his home the following evening, he called a porter to show us out.

"My family, especially my sons, will be excited to see two Americans," he said. "Be prepared! They will ply you with questions about Indians and wild animals. They have been reading books by your Mr. James Fenimore Cooper."

The exterior of Gottfried Mesner's house on Friedrichstrasse, with its gray stone facade and barred windows, looked so cold and uninviting as we stepped out of the cab and approached the steps that I feared we had let ourselves in for a cheerless evening, a dinner similar to ones I had known as a girl. The moment we passed through the heavy oaken door into the entryway, though, an air of warmth and happiness enveloped us. Someone was singing on the floor above, and the sound of laughter came from the back of the house as a smiling Gottfried welcomed us. His wife, Marthe, came bustling out to greet us, and within moments their four children were lined up to be presented. The two boys, Franz and Georg, I judged to be fifteen and sixteen, while the girls, Helena and Greta, were somewhat younger.

"And this is Tante Louisa, the one who knows all the family history," Gottfried said, leading us into the parlor where a slender, stiff-backed old lady sat close to a small coal fire. "She is the sister of my father; perhaps she knows something of his visit to your family."

"Yes, I know about everyone," the old lady said, smiling happily. "Who married whom, the names of their children, their birthdays; it is all in my head. But my nephew Gottfried tells me you inquire about my brother Hans, whom you call 'cousin.'"

"Yes, Fräulein Mesner," I said. "A Hans Mesner called on my father, John Ferguson, in New York some years ago, and we were told to address him as 'Cousin Hans.' "

"I do not understand." Tante Louisa frowned as she spoke. "Could there be another Hans Mesner? I do not know of one. My brother never mentioned such a visit, but then he was away frequently. No, he never mentioned the name Ferguson. As I told you, I remember all names, and I would know it if Hans had mentioned it to me."

"Who else was in your family besides you and Hans?" I asked.

"There were five of us, Ella, Magda and myself, besides the two boys."

"And did you have any cousins?"

"Oh, yes. We had cousins in Munich; their name was Reinholt, but there was no Hans in that family. Then there were the Mullers in Frankfort-am-Main. No Hans there, either. My sisters, Ella and Magda, both had only daughters, all grown now, with children of their own."

The old lady paused then, and sat as if deep in thought. "No," she said finally, "there is absolutely no Hans Mesner that I know of aside from my brother."

"What was the name of your other brother?" I asked after a moment or two.

"That was Philip," she answered with a frown. "He never married, and left home many years ago. He was drowned on his way to America. The captain of the *Ingrid,* one of my father's ships, wrote that he had no business being up on deck during a storm, but Philip was always headstrong, always knew what was best, and would do as he liked. Hans was more reasonable, and also more likeable. He all but worshiped Philip, would do anything for him. I never understood that . . . ."

At that point Marthe called us in to dinner, during which Dan was kept busy answering the young people's questions about life in America. They spoke almost no English, but Tante Louisa, whose knowledge of our language was excellent, acted as translator for me. When the meal was over I followed her out of the dining room, hoping to be able to talk further to her, but she excused herself politely, saying that at her age it was necessary for her to retire early. I was tired myself, and after a reasonable interval and promises to send the children picture postcards of New York, we took our leave.

"I don't know what to make of it," I said to Dan when we were on our way back to our hotel in the cab Gottfried had called for us.

"Well, obviously there was a Hans Mesner, Ellen, but if he visited you in New York he must have kept it a secret."

"And Papa acted so strangely when he was there. Oh, I simply don't understand it, and I'm sick and tired of the whole thing. I am not going to think about it anymore. What difference does it make what Mama said about Papa's name? None, none at all!"

I put the matter out of my mind for the rest of our trip, never giving it another thought until I was forced to report to Robert and Jay that I had accomplished nothing. Jay simply smiled and shrugged his shoulders, but Robert was disappointed and not a little annoyed. His health had deteriorated while we were gone, and shortly after our return he refused to leave his bed. He died one afternoon that fall while Will and I were sitting with him, a broken, unhappy man of fifty-eight.

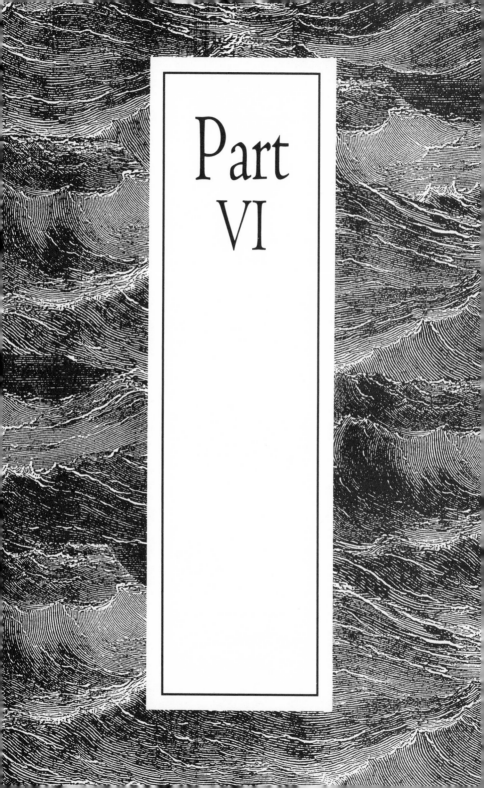

Part
VI

| Will |

When my mother and stepfather were abroad, my uncle Robert, after swearing me to secrecy, told me the real purpose of their trip. I couldn't take his story seriously, nor could I believe that my sensible, practical mother would give credence to the babbling of a dying woman about names and curses. Each time I stopped in to see him, though, my uncle harped on the same theme, dredging up past incidents and events that pointed to the fact that his name was not Ferguson. None of it seemed credible to me, but I tried to cheer him up by saying that if anyone could get to the root of the matter, my mother could. But, of course, she didn't.

She did, however, keep in touch with the Mesners over the years that followed her visit, and when I embarked for a year of study and research in Germany in June of 1876 I carried not only messages and letters, but also presents for each member of the Mesner family.

"A small return for their hospitality, Will," she said when I objected to the extra baggage. "You will see for yourself what good people they are. Now, remember, there are Gottfried and his wife, Marthe, and the children: Franz, Georg, Helena, and Greta. Then there's the aunt, the one they call Tante Louisa. She must be well on in years by this time. She speaks English, but some of the others do not—oh, I'm so glad you studied German, Will. Things will be easier for you there."

Tante Louisa, a fragile, bright-eyed woman, was indeed getting on in years, but old age was treating her kindly, allowing her to remain remarkably alert mentally, and as far as I could see, in good health physically. Gottfried and Marthe worried constantly that she might fall, but every time they suggested she use the cane they had bought she merely gave them a withering look.

"As if we proposed that she jump out of the window," Gottfried said with a sigh. "But she is not steady on her feet, Will. Maybe she will listen to you, since you are a physician."

I knew better than to try to persuade her; one glance at those sharp dark brown eyes and the determined set of her chin convinced me that bringing up the subject of the cane would only earn me one of the "withering looks." She did, however, consent to take Gottfried's arm when we were summoned to the dining room, her tiny figure in sharp contrast to his great bulk. I remembered that Ma had described him as being corpulent. Perhaps that was all he had been five years earlier, but in 1876 he was simply fat, enormously fat, due, no doubt, to the great quantities of heavy food he consumed. There again, I hesitated to interfere; I was, after all, a guest in the house, a frequent guest, I might add. I lived and worked at a hospital on the outskirts of Hamburg, but at the insistence of the hospitable Mesners most of my free time was spent in Friedrichstrasse.

Only the youngest of the children was at home at that time; the two boys were at the university at Heidelburg, and Helena, the older daughter, had married and gone to live in Bremen.

Greta, a pretty girl of eighteen with amazing deep blue eyes and masses of long blond hair, reminded me of my sister Fan, not so much in her appearance as in her personality and disposition. It was she who drew me back again and again on weekends, and by the time six months had elapsed I knew that I was, for the first time in my life, falling in love. I think Tante Louisa realized what was happening even before I did; I remember looking up from a chess game I was playing with Greta one afternoon and catching the old lady smiling across the room at us with an unmistakably knowing look in those still magnificent eyes. I smiled back at her, and later, when Greta was helping her mother put together a box of clothing for a poor family, I went over to talk to her.

"Tell me, Will," she said as soon as I was seated opposite her, "are you not, like me, one of five children?"

"There were five of us," I replied, "but two of my brothers were killed in the Civil War, so now we are only three."

"Ah, yes, I remember now. Your good mother even told me all your names: Philip, Rodney, John, Will, and Fanny. It was Philip and John who were killed, no? What was your brother Philip like? Was he warm and friendly?"

"Absolutely," I answered, thinking of Phil's outgoing, generous nature. "Everyone liked him; he made friends easily, and he was very well thought of in the import-export firm where he worked until the war came."

"Not like our Philip," she murmured, turning to look at the small coal fire, "who was also the oldest of five. No, not at all like him. Philip Mesner loved only himself, and maybe the girl he was courting. I do not know what became of her, but I doubt that she'd have been happy with him. He was a hard young man, very like my father. I remember thinking that he was becoming more and more like Father each day. Ah, it was so long ago . . ."

She sighed and sat back in the large armchair. "I think, though, that in spite of his personality my mother loved him sincerely—her firstborn, you know. She went into mourning for a full year when he was drowned. Perhaps my father mourned him, too, but I cannot be sure. He kept his emotions to himself. Ella and Magda and I were sorry that he died so young, but I think we were secretly glad it was not Hans to whom it happened.

"I talk too much of the past!" she exclaimed, suddenly sitting up straight and pointing to the fire. "A few more coals, Will, if you will be so good. Ah, that is better. Now, tell me about your work. Are you satisfied with our hospital here?"

Because of my wretched foot I had reached the age of thirty-two without ever having given serious thought to marriage. Nor, with the exception of my patients, had I had much contact with women, other than with those related to me. That was all changed, almost overnight, by my feeling for Greta. One moment I was picturing her delicate body in my arms, returning my love with a passion equal to my own, and in the next I could see her turning away from me, repulsed by my obvious deformity. A bittersweet summer that was, with happiness and despair constantly vying for supremacy in my being.

How could any woman, I asked myself over and over again, love a cripple encumbered with a heavy, built-up shoe? But then I would cheer up, and tell myself that Greta never so much as looked at my foot. And so it went, all that summer; when we strolled along the walk by the river in the evening her gait fitted itself to mine so unobtrusively as to make me feel that no conscious adjustment had been made. Without my asking she would take my arm, and as we sauntered down the path she would ask questions about life in America (she couldn't hear enough about my family and how we lived), or tell me about her activities of the past week.

I was surprised to learn that instead of staying home like most girls her age and occupying her time with household

174

chores and fancywork, she spent the greater part of each week-day in her father's office.

"It came about by chance, Will," she said with a little smile. "Mutti sent me there one morning with an envelope Papa had left on the breakfast table, and when I arrived at the office he was in a terrible state. The man who did the copy-ing, letters, manifests, and so on, was ill, and some papers had to go out at once, so I sat down and copied them. That is how it started. Now I do more than just copy; there is a small room, more like a closet, connected to the office, where for years papers and folders and records have been piled up helter-skelter. It takes forever to find anything, so I am working there now, putting things in order, first by the year, and then alphabetically."

"And you don't find it tedious work?"

"Far from it! Some of it is fascinating, Will. The names of the ships delight me, and the cargoes! Spices and things from places I've never heard of! I know I waste a lot of time poring over the old records, but it is fun, and then I do feel rewarded when I can help Papa lay his hands on something—he's really so apt to bumble about . . ."

Unlike you, my darling, I thought as we turned to retrace our steps.

It was on that homeward stretch on a still, cold day in early December, that the impossible happened. The heel of Greta's little fur-lined boot struck something—I don't know what—causing her to pitch forward, and she would have fallen head-long had I not caught her in my arms. She made no effort to pull away from the embrace in which I held her, and before I knew what I was doing I was raining long-held-back kisses on her eyes, her throat, and finally on her lips.

When I could speak I told her softly and slowly that I loved her, would always love her, and wanted to marry her, but felt that I had not the right to ask her.

175

"Why ever not, Will?" she asked, smiling, and putting her hand up to stroke my face.

I said nothing, but still holding her with one arm, pointed with my free hand to my foot.

She kept her eyes on my face, and shook her head slightly before speaking.

"You may not want to marry me when you know about my secret," she said sadly. She paused for a moment, and sighed deeply before continuing. "Have you ever noticed, Will, that all my gowns and dresses are made with long sleeves?"

I had paid little attention to her wardrobe other than to note that whatever she wore seemed to suit her slim form, and shook my head.

"I will show you why, then," she said, pushing up the sleeve of her fur coat and unbuttoning the cuff of her dress.

"It extends all the way up my arm," she said, revealing as much as she could of a long, reddish brown birthmark. "Up above the elbow, even."

Before she could cover it again I leaned over and kissed it gently. There were tears in her eyes when she looked up at me, and still there as we stood for some moments holding each other without speaking. There was no need for words.

I had known from the time of my arrival in Hamburg that the Mesners looked kindly upon me, and the way they continued to welcome me into their household was proof of that, but the genuine delight with which they welcomed me as a prospective son-in-law astonished me. Gottfried was exhuberant, Marthe was weepy, and Tante Louisa looked triumphant, as if she alone were responsible for the match. I rather think they had all worried that Greta was doomed to be a spinster forever, just as my family had assumed I would remain a bachelor.

"There is something you should know, Will," Gottfried said to me after the others had retired for the night and we lingered over a glass of plum brandy. "Marthe does not think I should mention it, but I would not feel easy in my mind if I withheld the information from you. It will probably make no difference to you, but I should not like to have you find it out later and feel that we had kept something hidden."

"What on earth—"

"Only Marthe and Tante Louisa and I know this, Will. Greta is not our daughter—no, wait, listen. She is the child of Marthe's sister, who died in childbirth. Her father, Heinrich Bauman, a soldier and a fine man, asked us to care for the baby until he could make a proper home for her. But that day never came; he was killed in a border skirmish when Greta was only two years old. We adopted her and made her our own, but she is not a Mesner by birth."

"And she doesn't know this? Your older children did not tell her?"

"They did not know themselves, nor do they now. They were all three quite young at the time, and simply thought of her as their baby sister."

"And you decided never to tell Greta?"

"It was Marthe's wish. She felt that Greta would have a happier life if she thought she had been born into the only family she knew, and that the birthmark was enough for her to bear. But now that you know, Will, do you still—"

"Still want to marry her? Of course I do! I love Greta for herself—I love her, love her! Whether she is a Mesner by birth matters not a bit. She means the world—"

"Then you will not tell her?"

"Certainly not. What would be the point? No, I give you my word that I shall never tell her."

Gottfried smiled and shook me by the hand. "You will make her happy, Will. I am certain of that, but you must promise to bring her back to see us from time to time. This house will seem empty without her."

Yes, the Mesners were delighted at the thought of a wedding, but of all those concerned my mother was the most joyful. She and Dr. Dan came over for the ceremony, which took place in July of 1877, and I doubt that she stopped beaming during their entire visit. She couldn't do enough, and in her generosity presented us with a honeymoon trip to Lake Como, invited us to stay with her in Washington Square until we found a residence, and promised to help Greta find her way around New York—anything she could think of that might give us pleasure.

I watched how tenderly she folded Greta in her arms when we were leaving for Switzerland, and every time I think of her smiling face as she stood on the sunlit platform waving to us, I remember how grateful I was a month later that she was back in New York when I found the answer to Robert's question.

We had intended to sail for America early in August, but Gottfried's sudden death shortly after our return from Lake Como delayed our departure for another six weeks. The morning the news came from the shipping office I was alone in the house except for the servants. Gottfried, of course, had left for the office, Greta and her mother had gone to the shops, and Tante Louisa had settled herself in a sunny spot in the garden in the rear of the house. I was preparing to organize my notes for a paper on the newest European methods of dealing with bone injuries when a distraught man I recognized as one of Gottfried's clerks burst into the room saying I was needed: Herr Mesner had collapsed while reading his mail.

I knew as soon as I saw him that Gottfried was beyond help; he had fallen forward across the huge table that served as his desk so that his head rested inches away from the last tray of coffee cake and strudel he would ever order.

During the difficult days that followed Gottfried's death I was full of concern for Greta's family—and for myself. Would

Marthe demand that her daughter give up her plan to live in America? Would Tante Louisa convince Greta that she was needed at home? Would I have to try to set up a practice in Hamburg? What would Greta do? To whom would she listen? Selfish of me, I know . . .

As it happened my worry was needless. A few days after the funeral, Marthe, pale but dry-eyed, announced that Gottfried's death should not affect our plans.

"You must have the life for which you have prepared yourself, Will," she said quietly but firmly, "and have Greta by your side. Georg and Franz will come home for good as soon as they finish at the university, and learn the business. You heard what Gottfried said in his will: They are to work under Herr Schmidt, who will be in charge until Franz is thirty years old. Then he will head the firm, and Georg will be second to him. Tante Louisa and I will just go on . . ."

She paused for a moment or two, as if trying to gather her thoughts, and then continued in the same low voice: "Greta, I want you—and take Will to help you—to go to Papa's office tomorrow. I know you have become familiar with it. You are to go carefully through his papers, and bring home to me any that are of a personal nature, letters that have nothing to do with the business."

"I have not seen any, Mutti," Greta said doubtfully, "but—"

"Nevertheless do as I ask, Liebchen. There may be letters from the boys, and greeting cards you children made for him when you were little. You know how Papa saved everything; he never threw anything away if he could help it."

Marthe was right. In an old cupboard in one corner of the little room we found dozens of greeting cards for birthdays, Christmas, and Easter, going back for more than twenty years, some of them laboriously handmade. There were also letters from Marthe and the children when they were away vacationing in the mountains or at the seashore. While Greta was sorting

179

these out at the large table in the adjoining room I picked up a worn leather case that had been half hidden beneath some old newspapers in the bottom of the cupboard. At first I thought it was empty, but a closer examination revealed that it contained four letters, written in German, still in their envelopes, and all addressed to Herr Hans Mesner. After a quick glance at the contents of one of them I refolded it, returned it to its envelope, and then put all four into my jacket pocket.

That night, when I was sure Greta was asleep, I slipped out of bed and went down to the empty dining room, where by the light of a single oil lamp I read through the small packet slowly and carefully. When I finished I sat for I do not know how long as one who has been asked to believe the impossible, knowing it must be true, but still unwilling to accept it. Then I wrote out a translation of each letter, secreted the entire packet in my medical bag, and went back to bed, but not to sleep.

By morning I had made up my mind that I was not in a position to decide whether or not to destroy the letters, and that my best course would be to do nothing until I had consulted with Jay.

Later on, after he had read my translations, Jay said he didn't know whether to be glad or sorry that I had made myself proficient in German.

"But that's beside the point, Will. We know now what my father was hiding; what do we do with that knowledge?"

In the end we did nothing except to agree that my mother should never see the letters. Jay said he'd keep them in a safe place, since neither one of us felt that they should be destroyed. They were, after all, a record of sorts (albeit a shameful one), and there was always the possibility, however remote, that there might be a need for them some day. I left them with Jay, glad to be rid of them, and went off to buy some flowers to take home to Greta.

———

180

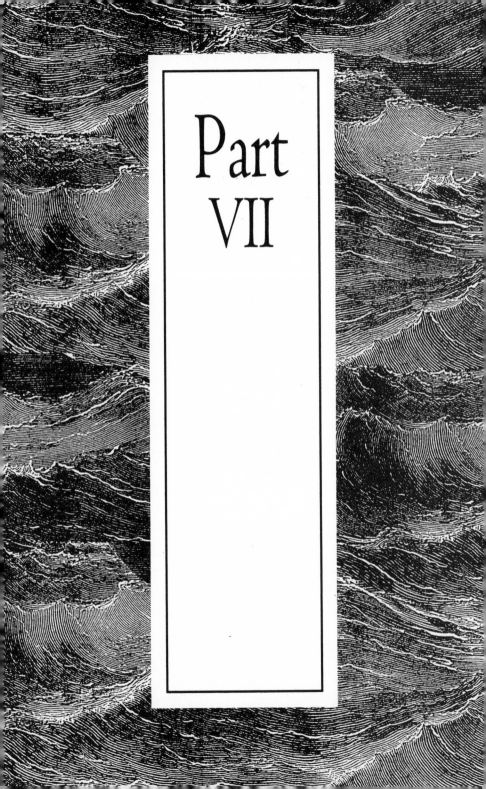

Part VII

Part
VII

1885

Ellen

Since a cold rain mixed at times with sleet and snow was falling on New Year's Day, Dan and I did not expect our customary number of callers. I knew better than to think Paul would venture out in such weather. To everyone's surprise my youngest brother had, as Dan put it, "decided to live," and became somewhat of a fanatic about his health. Rodney wouldn't be coming either; he had recently moved his family to Albany, to head up a branch office of his father-in-law's construction company, and Will sent word that he was on call at the hospital that day. I was thinking of how much T. F. used to enjoy the New Year's Day visitors when Dan spoke.

"It's a day to hug the hearth, dearest," he said, turning away from the window and picking up one of his medical journals. "I wouldn't count on anyone if I were you. What's that? Your writing desk? Good, bring it up close to the fire and keep me company while I catch up on the latest developments in patient care."

In spite of the weather and Dan's prediction, we did have three visitors: my darling Fan came in the morning to sit with us for over an hour, and in the afternoon, Jay's widow, Anne, appeared in time for tea. Then in the evening my nephew Alex arrived, looking very much like Robert at that age.

No one of them came empty-handed: Fan brought us a large box of Park and Tilford's fancy confections, and Anne presented me with a copy of Mr. Trollope's autobiography.

"I know how much you relished his novels, Ellen, and I thought you might enjoy reading about his own life. You might find it to your taste, too, Dan. And here," she added, opening her large reticule, "here is an envelope I found when we opened Jay's safe. I've been meaning to give it to you. It's marked 'Family Papers,' so obviously you are the one to have it, Ellen."

The envelope was sealed, so I put it aside to examine later.

"Jay must have intended to give it to you," Anne went on, making herself comfortable as she watched Bessie wheel in the tea trolley. "I suppose it slipped his mind, although it wasn't like Jay to forget things." She paused and waited for the maid to leave the room before continuing. "You know, Ellen, it's been two years now since he died, and I still miss him terribly."

"Of course you do, Anne—"

"It's strange," she interrupted, "that although I *do* miss him I am not really sad these days when I think of him. He was always so cheerful—and that's *how* I think of him. No wonder his patients loved him. He couldn't do enough for them, especially the poor ones. Oh, he never should have gone out on that last call! He had a cold and a cough, but would he stay in? No, of course not. If he had, he wouldn't have come down with pneumonia, but you knew Jay, Ellen."

"Indeed I did, Anne. Jay and I were close, very close. But this is interesting: Like yourself, I feel happy when I think of him, and sometimes find myself smiling at something he said or did years ago."

We were quiet while I poured the tea, and then Dan made Anne laugh by describing Jay and himself at the stage door of the Park Theater, waiting for a glimpse of Miss Fanny Kemble.

When it was time for her to leave, Dan saw her to the door—she wouldn't hear of his accompanying her the short distance to her house—and came back into the parlor looking thoughtful.

"She'll go on missing him," he said after a moment or two, "but she'll manage. She's a sensible woman."

I knew he was right, but my heart ached for her, as it had ached for myself after Ian's death.

Alex didn't bring a gift when he came that night—or did he? He strode into the parlor holding a package awkwardly done up in brown paper in both hands, and instead of offering it to me he sat down in front of the fire and began to unwrap it himself.

"I want you to have this, Aunt Ellen," he said, pushing the paper aside and holding up the Ship's Clock for me to see.

"How did you come by that, Alex?" I asked in astonishment. "I thought it was sold with everything else at the auction."

"It was supposed to be," he said, glancing rather sheepishly from me to Dan, "but I managed to hide it. Pa was furious with me at first, but later on he was glad. I was crazy about it when I was young, but I don't want it now. And I don't know what to do with it. I expect to be away from the city a good part of the time with this new assignment of mine, and I thought it would be safer with you than with my mother."

I nodded, understanding what he meant about Bettina, whom we seldom saw anymore. She is gradually slipping into senescence, but I am not unduly worried about her. Dan assures me that Harold Seabrook, whom she married a few years after Robert's death, sees that she has the best of care.

I didn't want the clock either, but Alex seemed so anxious for me to have it that I held out my hands to take it from him.

"This takes me back to times long before you were born, Alex," I said to cover my reluctance to accept his gift. "My father set great store by it."

"So did mine," he said with a slight smile. "When he was near the end he'd ask me to bring it in and put it where he could see it go through its paces. It was about the only thing that pleased him at the time."

"His memory went back, too, Alex," I said, placing the clock on the table next to my chair, and ringing for our evening cocoa. "But tell me about your new position."

His newspaper was sending him to the nation's capital, he said, for at least six months, and after that to Europe, either Paris or London.

"Ma made me learn French—oh, how I fought her over that—and I thought she'd be happy that her efforts were bearing fruit. But when I went to tell her that there was a good chance I'd be going to Paris she didn't even know me," he said, looking down at the carpet.

"She has some good days, Alex," Dan said carefully, "and maybe if you write to her from Paris . . ."

"I'll do that," he said, his face brightening, "and send her some French perfume—she'd like that."

He's a dear boy, and I shall miss having him drop in on us.

We retire early these days, so soon after he left I went up to bed, first putting the Ship's Clock on the mantel and glancing at Jay's envelope, which I decided to leave for the morning. And a good thing I did, too; had I opened it that night, sleep would have been out of the question.

Immediately after breakfast the next day I sat down at Dan's big desk and broke open the seal. Inside the envelope were four letters written in German, as well as a translation of each one, the latter written in what I recognized at once as Will's distinctive scrawl. My hand shook slightly as I put on my spectacles and began to read.

★ ★ ★

February 1, 1810
114 Hanover Square
New York, U.S.A.

My dear Hans,

This is just to let you know that I have arrived safely (contrary to anything you may have heard), and to give you my address. When I have more time I shall write at length. When you respond, please address the letter to John Ferguson, Esq.

Your brother,
Philip

March 30, 1810
114 Hanover Square
New York, U.S.A.

My dear Hans,

Forgive my long delay in writing to you. I have been busier than ever before in my life, and wished to wait until I had adequate time to tell you what has happened. But this is Sunday, and I have all day to myself.

Things have not worked out exactly as I planned before I left Hamburg. First let me tell you that the voyage on the *Ingrid* was a rough and stormy one. (Do not cross the Atlantic in winter if you can avoid it!) There were only a dozen passengers and the crew on board, and most of us were sick at least part of the time. When we were within two days of making port, my cabin mate, John Ferguson (he joined the ship when we

187

put in at Shannon), was washed overboard in towering seas that threatened to put an end to all of us.

Ferguson was a talkative chap, and during the long hours we spent lying in our bunks I learned a good deal about him. He and his brother had been orphaned as children, and taken in by an aunt and uncle, who had none of their own.

"No parents could have done more for two boys," he said, "than they did for us. But for them we'd have been put in an orphanage, or else become like the ragged street boys I used to see begging and thieving. You've no idea how many of them there are in Ireland, living on scraps and garbage, sleeping underneath wagons. A bloody shame it is. 'Twas the sight of them, I believe, that made me vow to feather my own nest with care."

He'd been educated at Trinity College in Dublin and was working in a bank when his uncle died (the aunt had succumbed to consumption a few years earlier), and he found himself with some capital.

"There wasn't as much as I'd thought there'd be," he said, "only about three thousand pounds after everything was settled, but that's enough to give me a start."

"What about your brother's share?" I queried.

Ferguson's expression clouded, and he did not reply at once.

"It is not easy for me to speak of Tim, Mesner," he said at last. "It is a hard and terrible thing to watch someone close to you go wrong, and that's what Tim did. Oh, it's a long story—"

He broke off and was silent for so long I thought he'd decided that he'd said enough.

"Anyway," he said with a sigh, "Tim did go wrong; he got in with a bad crowd, drinkers, carousers, and worse. They all were after money, and weren't particular how they came by it. Then one night Tim and a couple of others were nabbed for smuggling, caught in the act. They ended up being deported to Australia."

"And you never heard from him?" I asked.

"No, but Al Muldoon, one of that crowd, wrote from Sydney saying they'd arrived there. That's all; not another word."

Ferguson turned his face away from me then, and we were quiet. Later when I asked him why he left Ireland he said he saw no chance of making a fortune there, that America, with its rapidly growing industries, offered more opportunity. He was counting on his banking experience to help him establish a foothold in New York's financial sector, and had he lived, I'm sure he would have succeeded.

As I said, he was washed overboard. I remember that we were both feeling rotten that day. Toward evening he said that the air in the cabin was stale, and suggested that we go up on deck for a few minutes. It was a crazy thing to do; the wind was howling, and the seas were high enough to cause the ship to lurch from side to side.

"I'm going below!" I shouted to Ferguson, and turned back to the hatchway. Just then an enormous wave broke over the deck, setting it awash and knocking both of us off our feet. I caught hold of a windlass, and clung to it for dear life as the ship tilted frighteningly to starboard. Ferguson, who had been nearer the rail when he fell, caught hold of my foot, and in an effort to save himself, pulled me closer and closer to the rail. I was terrified; I couldn't let go of the windlass to extend a hand to him, nor could I pull him up with my foot. I heard him cry out seconds before another wave engulfed us, and when it receded he was gone. So were my spectacles.

In the relative calm that followed I struggled back to the passageway, and as I wrenched the hatch open I heard members of the crew shouting, "Man overboard! Herr Mesner overboard!"

At first I didn't realize that they thought I was the one to have drowned—I was somewhat groggy from what I'd been through, and it seemed as if my entire face was on fire from where I'd scraped it on the deck when I fell. It wasn't, therefore, until I was back in the cabin, lying exhausted in my bunk, that it dawned on me that here was a God-given opportunity to assume a new identity. Let them think Philip Mesner had drowned! From that moment on I would be John Ferguson! And I would have his three thousand pounds! He'd left no relatives who could expose me, so I would be perfectly safe. I got up from the bunk and stared at myself in the mirror. My face was a bloody mess, and hurt like hell, but I wasn't thinking of that then. I was busy comparing my appearance with Ferguson's. His eyes were blue, quite dark, and mine, as you know, are brown, but aside from that we were not unlike in looks. We were approximately of the same age, height, and girth; we both had dark hair, as well as beards that needed trimming by a professional. Neither of us had attempted to shave during the voyage; it would have been disastrous. Another point in my favor: This was not the first time members of the crew had taken one of us for the other. There should be no trouble, I told myself, in passing for my unfortunate traveling companion.

I lay down on my bunk again, and was almost asleep when I suddenly remembered that Albert Pfeil would be at the dock in New York to meet me—Father had told me to expect him—and I had to make sure the old man did not recognize me. I regretted the loss of my spectacles, and was wondering how best to disguise myself when someone knocked on the cabin door. Before I could call out that I wanted nothing, the bos'un, who took care of injuries sustained aboard ship, came in and set to work examining my scrapes, cuts, and bruises.

"A right good job you did on your face, Mr. Ferguson," he said, opening a small wooden chest containing medical supplies. "Doesn't look too serious, though. Needs cleaning up, and a bit of bandaging. Painful, eh?"

I simply nodded, afraid to speak for fear he'd detect my German accent. When he finished cleansing and binding up my wounds, he stood back and grinned at me.

"I doubt that your own mother would recognize you now," he said cheerfully. "No, don't get up. Lie still for a while, and leave the bandages on for a week at least. You should be fine by then."

After he left I arose and studied my face (what I could see of it) in the mirror again. Plasters of some sort covered most of my nose and both cheeks, and my forehead was hidden under a large bandage that encircled my head. I looked as if I had had the worst of it in a brawl, but I was almost deliriously happy. It would take someone more astute than Albert Pfeil to penetrate this disguise!

I kept to my cabin for the short remainder of the voyage, speaking to no one, just nodding when the captain or one of the officers came to inquire about my health, and arrived in New York as John Ferguson. I wore his clothes and carried his satchel, as well as the smaller case containing his money, which he had kept under his bunk. The satchel presented no problem, but I had not the tools to force the lock on the case, the key to which I had seen on the chain Ferguson wore around his neck, and which now lies on the ocean floor. I made a thorough search of the cabin to see if I could find a letter I had seen him writing, but without result. I shall not worry about that; his only relative was a brother in Australia, and he is thought to be dead.

My own possessions, with the exception of one important object, I left for the authorities to find. They will assume that any money I had went into the sea with me, so of course I took the two hundred marks Father gave me. *I* assume that the captain of the *Ingrid* has notified him of my death. Do not disillusion him!

Have I not been clever, Hans? Ah, the dinner gong has sounded; I shall write again.

Your brother,
Philip

One last note: Albert Pfeil never even looked at me when I passed within ten feet of him on the dock! When I looked back he was going on board the ship, to be informed of my death, no doubt.

May 30, 1810

My dear Hans,

Getting a business started is not easy, and it is also time-consuming. I am going into partnership with Otis Lamb, who has had some experience in shipping. Our firm will be known as Ferguson and Lamb, and in time I may put the Ship's Clock in a place of honor in my office!

Of course you must have guessed what happened to it, but I'll give you the details. I knew that since the *Ingrid* was to sail at six o'clock in the morning you and Papa and I would go directly from the house to the ship, and that you two would return home for breakfast before going to the office. Therefore, the night before on my way home from saying farewell to Maria, I paid a last visit to the offices of Mesner and Sons, and secreted the clock under my coat.

I had to have it, Hans. You will remember how fascinated I was by it all my life, won't you, and how I made little replicas of the ship? Some of them were good enough that Herr Schaefer was able to sell them for me. Some day, when I am old and finished with business, I shall make an exact copy of the ship, complete with a working clock. I have ideas for other inventions as well, but just now the shipping business takes all my time.

I do not consider that I stole the clock, Hans, since Grossvater told me long ago that it was always handed down to the oldest son. I merely claimed my inheritance a bit early. It is here on my table as I write this, and I shall keep it until it is time to give it to my firstborn son.

About the stove: I deliberately smashed some of the tiles, the ones that show Solomon looking as if he's about to cut the baby in half. I did this for two reasons: first, out of anger at Father, and second, in the hope that he would think robbers or drunken louts had broken in. I tossed ledgers and papers around to make it look as if they were searching for money, and I sincerely hope my ruse worked.

Perhaps I am wicked, Hans, but I cannot help but chuckle every time I picture Father's wrath when he discovered the chaos in his precious office!

Enough for the present. Keep remembering to address your letters to John Ferguson. I probably should have taken a different name once I was off the ship, but I didn't think of that until after I'd gone into business with Otis Lamb, by which time it was too late to change.

Your brother,
Philip

233 Broadway
New York, U.S.A.
August 30, 1835

My dear Hans,

First, let me say that you wasted your time coming here this summer to try to persuade me to return to Hamburg now that Father is dead. I shall never go back, nor will any member of my family set foot in that city. It would be too complicated to become Philip Mesner again. I know, Brother, that your old affection for me, as well as business with the Wilkins Brothers, led you to make the trip, but you must understand that I cannot do as you ask.

Second, and more important, you will remember that while you were here I requested that upon your return to Hamburg you would burn any letters I wrote you after I arrived in this country. At the time I did not explain why in case Maria should overhear, and I did not want to worry her.

This is the reason: Timothy Ferguson, the long-missing brother of my cabin mate on the *Ingrid,* has turned up here looking for his brother, John, in order to claim his rightful share of the money left by their uncle. He came to see me, but he knew immediately that I was not his man because of the color of my eyes. He does not know that I have made use of his inheritance, but *you* know. BURN THOSE LETTERS! And let me know that you have done so. If my imposture is discovered I shall be ruined for life, and I will go to any lengths to keep that from happening.

This Timothy Ferguson does not come alone; he has a son, Ian, and I shall see to it that neither one of them has anything to do with members of my family. *Anything.* Who knows what papers or records they may have that might cause my exposure? That letter that I couldn't find, the one I saw John Ferguson writing in the cabin of the *Ingrid,* may have fallen into their hands. I must find a way to examine their papers—but how?

If I am found out, all I have worked for will come to naught, and I shall be disgraced. I live in constant fear of that. Some days I think I am going mad. Let me hear from you immediately, Brother, saying you have done as I ask.

Philip

★　★　★

Will	"You were never supposed to see those letters, Ma," I said when I stopped in at the Washington Square house the day after New Year's. "But of course Anne couldn't have known that."
	"You and Jay had the best of motives, Will dear," she said unemotionally. "You were trying to spare me, and I appreciate that. But—now, don't be astonished at what I am about to say—just listen. I never liked my father. As a child I was terrified of him, and as a woman I came to dislike him intensely.

After reading these letters, which reveal him as an amoral, wicked man as well as a thief, I feel that my dislike has been justified. It is possible that he was responsible for Ian's death, that he killed him himself with his cane. He was capable of terrible deeds. Perhaps he was accursed after all, but only by himself, not by his father. Or maybe he did go mad . . .

"The letters have not upset me as much as you might think. In fact, they have clarified things for me. And, strangely enough, now that I know the truth, the strong dislike I felt for Papa has been partly replaced by pity, pity for a man who so misused his talents. It is ironic, isn't it, that the man he impersonated was just as much a scoundrel as he was himself? You must see, Will, that the real John Ferguson, the one who was drowned, the one who was responsible for T. F.'s being deported to Australia, was completely dishonorable; a liar and a thief. That's all very clear now."

She sighed, and looked thoughtfully down at the letters on the table next to her chair. "I wonder," she said slowly, "what happened to the rest of the correspondence between Papa and Cousin Hans? There must have been more letters written over the years. Why are these the only ones to survive?"

"Hans probably did burn the others, Ma," I answered, "and these escaped because he'd put them away in the bottom of the cupboard for safekeeping, and then forgot about them. I've told you how disorderly Gottfried was about his papers. Maybe Hans was like him in that."

"I think that's what happened," Dr. Dan said, getting up to tend the fire.

"What makes you say that, Dan?" my mother asked.

"Well, I don't know how orderly Hans was, but from all accounts he was extremely fond of Philip—devoted to him, in fact—and I do not believe he would have kept the letters deliberately when Philip had asked him so forcefully to burn them."

My mother nodded, and sat quietly for a few moments. "I wonder," she said musingly, "how this knowledge would have affected Robert? Maybe it's just as well he died without knowing the truth about Papa."

"It might have caused another stroke," I said. "But what about T. F.? How would he have reacted?"

"It's difficult to say—" Dr. Dan began.

"Oh, no, it isn't, Dan," my mother interrupted. "It's not difficult at all—at least not for me. T. F. would have been shocked, of course, but he would have been relieved that nothing *he* had done was the cause of Papa's antipathy. That was what bothered him all those years—that he didn't know. And he'd done nothing."

"Of course you're right, Ellen. T. F. was such a fine character that in time he would have forgiven your father for his imposture, and even forgiven the debt of three thousand pounds."

"I don't know about the money, Dan, but I do know he wouldn't have made a fuss. Oh, I do miss him! He was such a dear man, and so good to us for such a long time."

She held a handkerchief up to her eyes for a moment, and then glanced up at the Ship's Clock, which was striking five.

"I know that I'll burn the letters, but I do not know what I'll do with the clock. Alex gave it to me, and I do not want it."

"What do you think you will do with it, Ma?"

"I'm not sure. Do you want it, Will? No? Then I shall have to think about it. Perhaps a collector of antique clocks would be interested in it. Oh, I just don't know!"

Several months passed before the subject of the clock came up again. Since it was not on display in the parlor of the Washington Square house, I assumed that because it brought back too many unpleasant memories my mother had put it out of sight and might simply leave it hidden away. I was surprised, therefore, when Dr. Dan opened the door for me one evening in September and greeted me with the news that the fate of the Ship's Clock had been decided.

"It has taken your mother a long time to make up her mind, Will," he said, letting me into the hallway, "but she has, I am convinced, come up with the best possible solution."

"Oh, Will dear!" my mother exclaimed, rising from her chair to hug me. "I'm so glad you've come. I've decided what to do with the clock, and I am happy about it. At first I thought

197

I might donate it to a museum, but when Greta told me that you and she were planning to take little Frederick to visit the Mesners at Christmas—"

"You want me to return the Ship's Clock to them? But how will I explain—"

"I've thought of that, too," she said, her eyes shining with pleasure. "You need not explain anything at all. Tante Louisa would be the only one to know anything about the clock, and she is gone now. So, you see, it will simply be a Christmas present, an appropriate one for the mantelpiece in the home of shipping merchants!"

I did as she requested, but the Ship's Clock was not destined to grace a mantelpiece. The last time I saw it, it was standing at the end of the long wooden table Franz and Georg used as a desk in the old-fashioned office of Mesner and Sons on the Hafenplatz.